PRINCE OF

ENVY

PRINCES OF SIN:
SEVEN DEADLY SINS SERIES

K. ELLE MORRISON

This novel is a work of fiction. All characters and events portrayed are products of author's imagination and used fictitiously.
Editing by Caroline Acebo
Proofreading by Norma's Nook Proofreading
Cover Designed by Cassie Chapman at Opulent Designs
Interior page design by K. Elle Morrison

Kellemorrison.com

Print ISBN: 979-8-9887063-7-3
Ebook ISBN: 979-8-9887063-8-0

This one is for those who are braver than they think.

DEAR READERS

Please read carefully

This book contains material that may be considered inappropriate for readers under the age of 18.

These materials cover:

Elements of religious trauma, alcohol, and graphic language. Graphic sex between consenting adults but also SA and gore ON PAGE.

Your mental health is so important. There will be a notice within the pages to direct you back to this warnings page for a synopsis. The sensitive material discussed and displayed may trigger some readers who have experienced SA, spousal abuse, or assault at the hand of a partner or friend.

If you or someone you know is experiencing domestic violence or abuse please consider reaching out to the National Domestic Violence Hotline 1-800-799-7233 https://www.kellemorrison.com/trigger-warnings-synopsis-1

OTHER TITLES BY K. ELLE MORRISON

To stay up-to-date on upcoming titles, bonus material, advanced reader opportunities, and so much more visit Kellemorrison.com to join the newsletter!

For all upcoming projects and updates from K. Elle Morrison please subscribe to the *FREE* Newsletter!

Kellemorrison.com
Linktree

CHAPTER I
CELESTE

I hadn't meant to summon a real demon. The Ouija board was pink, for fuck's sake!

The planchette I'd found in that blasted book had lifted off the board and spun in circles until the incantation I'd been repeating was done. With a hollow thud, it fell onto the cardboard, and the room swelled around me.

A menacing presence had answered my call, and when he appeared, my thick-headed self stayed still while every one of my self-preservation-having friends ran as fast as their fluffy socks could take them up the basement stairs.

I wasn't brave or dimwitted. I was scared shitless and frozen in place when he stepped out of the shadows, gruesome, decaying, and reeking of death. The smell was so putrid that it choked the scream in my throat.

With each step, he grew taller until he was a jagged

cliff that impaled anything that dared climb it. Haunting and treacherous, he cocked his head down at me, still on my knees. My legs were useless sausages.

"Speak, human," he demanded. His voice was salt on raw skin.

"I-I . . ."

My friends' screams from the upper levels of the house were muffled by the being in front of me. The being we had brought through what Ellen called "the void."

"Your courage has gone, and your spine is as feeble as reeds. But you have summoned greatness. Do not squander it."

He had reached out a corroded skeletal hand and lifted my chin until I was forced to my feet. He was still over a foot taller than me.

One second, I was swallowing down his rancid, hot breath, and the next, an impossibly beautiful man stood in the monster's place.

Judging books by their covers was part of my job, and this creature with savage power was evil incarnate. Something about him reached deep inside of me and fomented every dark thought I'd ever had to my surface. Sins that I'd committed pooled in my belly to stir and ripple at the gentle caress of his fingers down my throat.

"Name." Another demand from him, but his voice was as smooth as silk in this new form.

"Celeste."

His gaze on mine was detrimental. If he pulled

away, I would die of suffocation. My lungs would scramble to follow him, but only after my pounding heart had broken free of the prison within my ribs. He was life and death and all that was in between.

"My Celeste." His fingers embraced the column of my neck, a perfect fit.

"Yes."

Of course I was his. Right?

I'd called upon him from that blasted book I'd found in the archives. The one I was supposed to have brought to my professor but had said was missing instead.

It had called to me. I'd felt it. When I picked it out of the stacks, it wrapped me in a sensation that I could only describe as *home*. Written just for me.

That was all clear to me now, in this moment, with his hand around my throat and his eyes so heated that I was going to melt into a puddle at his feet, then apologize for staining his soles.

I'd brought it to the party to show my friends and fellow occult-loving weirdos. To show them the meticulous journaling of a sixteenth-century priest who'd documented every exorcism he'd performed down to the color of the vomit each victim expelled.

What I hadn't expected was for Laura to have brought a novelty Ouija board from the kink shop where she worked. The glitter penises between letters and numbers showed it was a bachelorette party gag gift. It had even come with a list of questions to ask "the beyond" about your future husband. We'd taken turns asking the spirits about our partners or some-where-out-there soulmates.

When it was my turn, all hell had broken loose.

Literally.

My body had been taken over so easily by some unknown force. I'd had the priest's diary on my lap for safekeeping when words formed on my tongue and began twisting into phrases that sounded like Latin or Aramaic, a mix at my best guess. Languages I could decipher but could not speak in conversation.

"Please." I didn't know what I was asking, but he did.

"Don't be frightened, my gift," he said, his low voice a whisper feathering over my lips. "I have been waiting for you."

"For me?" I breathed.

"You freed me." His sincere gratitude was melodic. Bells and harps sang behind his words only to crash to silence in the pauses we shared. "I am in great debt to you for ending my solitude."

"But I didn't do anything." I tried to reason with myself more than the demon I had inadvertently been carrying around with me for weeks.

"Celeste, ask for whatever your heart desires. Wish it and I'll make it so."

The space between our bodies was beginning to hurt. The tiny hairs along my spine rose and my skin ached to be touched. My fuzzy, jumbled mess of a brain reached for any desire outside of wanting him to rip my clothes off and do unspeakable things to me for hours.

Clarity would not come, but greed did.

"The fellowship. I want the first pick of the cultural anthropology fellowship."

It sounded small in comparison to what he was offering. I imagined, if I had thought of it, the demon would have given me the world on a platter. But the fellowship had been my goal for the last six years. All of my postgrad work had been solely focused on the opportunity to join some of the brightest minds who were rewriting history as we knew it with technology that would give Malinowski wet dreams.

I was in the running, but the choice hadn't been made yet, and the candidates were just as, if not more, impressive than me.

I had no plan B.

"Speak my truest name and it is yours."

His truest name. How was I supposed to know that?

No sooner had the confusion clouded my mind than my lips formed the syllables, the taste of them stinging and scratching to the tip of my tongue.

"Vassago."

CHAPTER 2
VASSAGO

Celeste was my reward. A gift created and given to me by our Father for all His years of mistreatment and dissolution. I was once one of His most loved sons. Back when He was feared. Vengeful. A wrathful Creator who doled out punishments to His children in spades.

When we were driven beneath His heel in exile, I knew one day He would realize the mistake He made and bestow the most precious offering to win over my favor.

Celeste was that and so much more.

There was nothing short of magic lurking under her skin. Her voice was the most powerful command. Every nerve, cell, molecule in my being answered to the slightest hum of her breath.

When she moved, each cord of her muscles strummed the blood through my veins. The pump of

7

her heart was reason alone for my eyes to open and endure another day on this plane.

Her mere existence was messianic. A prophecy promised unto me and fulfilled in the purest form of glory. Not a day ended without the pleonectic need to taste her flesh on the tip of my tongue like ambrosia. Carnal desire to sink my teeth into her while I senselessly ravaged her consumed me. My desperation to be close to her wouldn't be sated until my heart beat within her chest and hers in mine.

The moment my true name left her delectable lips, there had been a resonating confirmation that no one else would own her the way I would. We belonged together, and eventually, she would see it too. The itch was there. The mutual connection of our souls wasn't only in the deal we'd struck. Her pupils gobbled me up, and her body responded so easily to my touch.

She couldn't rid herself of me. Not in any aspect of the concept. Our souls were intertwined in a tight weave, and I would never allow anything to sever that bond, not even her fear. It would be natural to fear such an engulfing presence. A fate so grand that it would threaten to burn her from her soul to her fingertips.

Without a doubt in the grand design, Celeste would sit upon my throne with a sea of blood and broken bones at her feet. My altar. Mine to worship, and the world's to fear.

The one being I knew who would be able to help see my vision become a reality was across the country but a small step through the dark, sucking void between time and space.

The apartments above The Deacon were occupied by those Sitri saw fit. I could feel the presence of more than just demons lurking beyond the door of Sitri's penthouse. I knocked softly at first, unsure if he would even welcome a visit from me after all my time away.

After no answer, I pounded my fist over and over.

"All right!" Sitri opened the door wide, and his expression melted from anger to something else. Pity? "Vassago?"

"Hello, brother." I smiled and walked into his home.

"Where have you been? No one has heard from you in—"

"Fifty years. Almost fifty-one. I was trapped in a human board game."

Sitri's jaw dropped. "You're kidding."

I was, sort of. The item I had been trapped in wasn't original to the sparkly penis Ouija board, but it was still part of the reason I had been able to be released. That and Celeste's ability to read the dead language that had bound me.

All information that Sitri didn't need right now.

"I was saved and want to return the favor. But for that, I need your help." I encapsulated my tale to him while I rummaged through his shiny stainless-steel refrigerator and took out an apple.

He paled slightly. I took a bite from the fruit and savored the tart and sweet notes. I added apples to the list of things that had changed while I was gone, along with streetlights and traffic signs. No longer was there only one type of red, waxy apple with dry, mealy flesh.

"Vass, you've been gone a long time," Sitri said. "Things aren't the way they used to be. I am not as powerful as I once was. I will do my best, but I can't promise you the outcome you might be hoping for."

I didn't know what I was hoping for or if Sitri would truly be able to give it to me.

What I did know was that the Prince of Lust was reliable and our influences on human minds often correlated for more dramatic outcomes. Leaders of the world had crumbled under lust and envy. Ours was the touch that could make mountains move and seas wither to piles of salt. The mixture turned what could be seen as pleasure into obsession. Obsession was easily influenced into destruction and chaos.

Perhaps on a smaller scale, his help paired with mine would be enough to clear the way for Celeste to achieve her dream, though inspiring her lust would also benefit me. But the look Sitri was giving me said more than he wished. He couldn't help me because he wasn't able, not because he didn't want to.

I watched his shoulders slump as he wandered around his kitchen and checked the hall for any eavesdropping beings. I couldn't pinpoint the third supernatural presence in the vicinity, but I didn't doubt Sitri had known it carnally.

"My influence has been lacking," he finally said, dropping his head in unwarranted shame.

"I'm waiting for a riveting explanation." I dipped

my chin to meet his eyes when he finally looked up. "And remember that I haven't had a real conversation in half a century, so spare no unsavory detail."

He made a sound that should have been a humorous laugh, but it was heavy with loss and regret.

"A tale for another time. But the bottom line is that I haven't been able to perform my tried-and-true powers over others in a long time. So, unless you're wanting me to extend an invitation to one of the most exclusive clubs in L.A., I don't know what I can offer you, brother."

I waited for a secondary option, but it didn't come. "I don't believe Celeste would be impressed with The Deacon. No offense."

"None taken." He gave a real laugh this time. "You must be very grateful to Celeste to come and request a favor."

My mouth spread in a smile that even surprised me. Grateful? I was grateful to the sun for existing for as long as it had just so her soul could bless this plane. I was grateful to the hundreds of ancestors she had that carried her DNA until her conception.

I was more than grateful. I was devoted.

"I would bring her the moon if she wished for it. But all she wants is to fulfill a dream. My influence is powerful, but not the right kind for what I want to accomplish. I was hoping to cause a great deal of lust-filled scandals to pave the way for her to win out on her ambitions."

I tossed the core of the apple into the sink and leaned my hands on the counter behind me.

He narrowed his eyes. "Why?"

"She was made for me. Every speck of her being was gathered from the reaches of the universe into a soul that has been promised and presented for my repentance."

The power of that proclamation swelled in my chest and caught into a burning fire of need to touch her as soon as I possibly could.

He nodded but didn't question me. "Then you know what she desires. You don't need my influence or help."

Sitri was right. The vibration behind my skin beckoned me to show her that I was what she needed. I looked down the slope of my body and at the hard muscles that stretched the fabric of my T-shirt. Each one was at her disposal for whatever whim she wished. I just had to be there at the right moment.

I took a breath and was about to step through the void when my ears perked at a sound coming from down the hall.

"Vassago?" It was Sitri's angel, Ezequiel.

"Watcher." I acknowledged him with a nod.

Sitri and Ezequiel's relationship was detested by other demons. Watcher Angels were said to be the cowards who refused to fall with the rest of us. They only made their intentions clear afterward, breeding humans like cattle and living among them like kings. There were tales and humors that demons would spin and spread like thin veils of silky disdain. Jealousy was at the root of all those misgivings. Envy that the Watchers remained holy in their own way while the rest of the Fallen had had to watch our abilities rust into broken shards of their former glory.

I, on the other hand, understood Watcher Angels. Maybe more now that I had been given my own human gift. If any of them had a fraction of the love for their human that I held for Celeste, then drowning the Earth for them would have been more than worth the atrocities.

"I have to go, but you owe me a titillating story and a drink," I said to them and turned to the door.

Sitri stopped me at the threshold and pulled me into a tight embrace. I wrapped my arms around him to feel his heart beating within him.

Broken but still fighting for peace. A trait I would always admire in the Prince of Lust.

CHAPTER 3
CELESTE

T he library on campus opened at seven thirty in the morning, but all the good tables were often gone by nine. So, with my arms full of books —and hands clutching my latte—I pushed open the door and stepped into the empty entryway. The atrium was still unlit, but the domed glass ceiling was filling the space with golden sunlight.

Janie, the morning librarian, gave me a quick glance of acknowledgment then a wave over the top of her newspaper.

"Morning," I called as my feet quickened up the first flight of stairs.

The fourth floor was where my favorite scholarly tomes slumbered. I spent most of my time digging through the archives for clips of details to be sifted through and referenced in whatever paper I was working on. Some would say my major was boring, but the thrill I got from hunting for information in the towers of books was similar to climbing mountains. Years could go by without some of these books being touched, but they were impregnated with voices of wisdom from the past.

This week, I was hunting for what recent aspect of human history that would cause someone to hide a demon-possessed planchette in the rare *Malleus Maleficarum*. The game instrument had been tucked in the pocket on the back cover for long enough to leave a permanent indentation in the pages. It hadn't been alone in being a misplaced item that called the yellowed pages its burial ground.

Glued into the first chapter of the book was an envelope that held a ring of rusted keys inscribed with a series of unknown etchings. The editorial notes that categorized the contents described many of the items as of unknown origin or collection date. It was more like the book had been tucked into the library's rare catalog for safekeeping and not for education.

Of all the hidden gems that dwelled in the stacks, the book had been the center of my interest for the last couple weeks. If I hadn't been Dr. Hou's TA, the sequence of events that led to a demon from Hell stalking me wouldn't have occurred.

I wasn't exaggerating. Vassago had been following me everywhere I went for days. I could feel his tall frame lurking in dark corners, see him out of the corner of my eye, but he vanished when I dared to look. In conversations with my peers, I could see their skin break out in goose bumps as they searched the room for the presence of evil that had brushed over their senses.

The initial fear had subsided into general unease after the shock had worn off, but a newly summoned shadow was keeping his distance. I was in a constant state of waiting for the moment when he finally decided to show himself.

What had started as uncomfortable was becoming familiar and safe. Walking to my car late at night didn't send anxiety into my belly because I knew that the feeling of being watched was valid. More than once, I'd thought about speaking his name. He wasn't going to hurt me, I'd told myself, because he'd had ample opportunity to kill me. I didn't know what he wanted, but I was too scared to ask.

So as I flipped through the pages of another account of the practice of exorcism in the 1660s, I had the distinct feeling of someone reading over my shoulder.

I turned the pages of the history book slower than normal. Having an accelerated reading speed was natural to me, but it was anyone's guess as to how fast Vassago was reading through the same passages.

When I finally got to a section about the tools of certain rituals, I saw a small diagram in the corner depicting a crude Ouija board. The planchette's definition and estimated date of creation were bulleted next to it.

I shoved my hand into my jacket pocket and pulled out the planchette that might have been Vassago's prison

—or the key to his freedom. I wasn't sure which was the truth yet. I turned it over in my hand then brought it closer to my face. Several etchings in the old, stained wood created a pattern that resembled a boxy beetle with pincers and a double-curved tail. It was worn and rubbed almost completely off. It was the only spot on the implement that seemed to have gotten attention from whoever had owned it. The polished edges and painted decorative bits were almost brand new in comparison.

The questions buzzing through my brain were deadened by a chill that ran up my spine when what felt like a hand gripped my shoulder, and the shell of my ear warmed as if his breath were whispering the answer I craved. I let my shoulders melt and my head loll back. There wasn't a solid form there, but the air felt thick, soft, and warm against my scalp.

A pressure on the back of my hand led me to touch my stomach and push up the hem of my shirt to expose my belly. Then, an unseen tug at the waist of my jeans made my breath hitch. My skin heated under the invisible force as it made itself at home between my thighs. It—no, I pulled my legs apart. The hand at my navel moved down and into my silky panties. I would never touch myself in public, but this wasn't me—was it?

My lips silently framed the syllables of his name and a plea for him to stop. That was what I wanted after all. For the evil creature I'd unleashed onto the world to stop turning me into a puddle of need when I thought about him for too long.

I swallowed hard and pulled my hand away. I wasn't going to give in to whatever game he was playing. The choking air in my throat thinned, but the low hum of something sinister in the stale room sounded like the rasp of my name.

I strained my ears hard to hear past the stillness of the books for any resonance.

"You've beat me here again." A very real voice shocked me from my trance and pushed the pressure from my shoulder.

I straightened my spine and pulled down my shirt to erase the proof of my momentary weakness.

It was Liam, my research partner. He was too tall and muscular for a scholar, but he was a beautiful sight. He let his backpack fall off his shoulder then plopped down in a seat at my table.

"Of course I did," I quipped, not bothering to look up from the pages to meet his inevitably offended expression. "You had to make your latest bed companion breakfast before meeting up."

Liam had a body count a mile long, and his bedpost was a pile of wood chips at this point.

"You've wounded me," he answered with all the drama of a lost theater major. "As if I allowed her to spend the whole night. You know that honor is only for you if you ever see me fit."

I rolled my eyes and finally closed the history book with a satisfying thud. "You're such a slut, Liam. I know I'm just a challenge you haven't won."

"Your boyfriend is the challenge." He wagged a finger at me. "You are the prize, darling."

The pink on my cheeks encouraged him far too much. Harmless flirting wasn't cheating on Duncan, I knew that. But if he ever heard Liam give me this sort of attention, he would volunteer every reason under the sun as to why I was no prize.

"Anyway"—I pushed three books from the table into Liam's lap—"help me bring these downstairs. The coffee bar will be opening soon, and I need my second jolt before our first class."

"I am here to be used by you." He gave me an exaggerated bow of his head before picking up both of our bags and the pile of books.

I shook my head and made my way down the first flight of stairs.

"What did you end up doing last night?" he asked from behind me. "You were here when I left at ten o'clock."

"The usual." I took the corner down the second flight of stairs before continuing, "Researched until closing, drove home while listening to a murder podcast, got home in time to call Duncan to tell him goodnight, studied until my eyes ached, then studied some more."

Duncan was gone for over a week on a trip to the archives at Boston University, and if I were being honest, I was glad he hadn't been around while I got a grip on the monster who'd almost inspired me to make a mess of myself in public.

"I hope Duncan told you to hydrate and made you

take a short fuck break when he got home." He chuckled, but I cringed internally.

On the outside, Duncan and I look like the perfect academic couple. We met in graduate school, moved in together after six months, and had been applying for the same grants and internships ever since. But at home, Duncan could be abrasive. I never seemed to do the right things or say what he wanted to hear. When we both applied to the fellowship, he'd mocked the font I used for my entry essay. When his words finally brought me to tears, he held me close and promised that when he got the fellowship, he would help me during next year's round.

I knew he was sort of an asshole, but he was my biggest supporter when it came to my studies. His brain was a sponge and took very little exposure to retain information that took me days to memorize. He also was caring and a great cook when he wanted to be.

"He hasn't come home from Boston yet. He'll be back on Sunday. But I made tea before I went to bed," I assured him.

Liam scoffed. "I'll remind him in stats next week that tea doesn't do the same as a good romp in the sack." He took extra steps to overtake me on the last flight down.

"Please don't. You know he doesn't like it when other people comment on our relationship."

Liam was the type to make a joke out of things but not accept the consequences if they went awry. Playfully expressing to Duncan that I needed a good fucking would be enough to set him off for days. He was the jealous type on a level that at times felt overboard. But it was better than being with a man like Liam, who didn't recognize when a joke had been beaten to death.

"I won't ruffle Duncan's precious feathers." Liam rolled his too-blue eyes then spun around with his face turned up to the gorgeous glass above. "But if you get lonely this weekend, you know who to call."

He winked, but I didn't answer.

I often wondered what type of woman Liam was actually interested in or if it mattered at all as long as they had a hole for him to stick his dick into. He had several dating apps on his phone and always seemed to have someone lined up for the evening. When I asked too many questions, I would get answers like, "Her husband is cheating on her so she thought a hookup with a younger guy would be a good way to get back at him." Or, "We hooked up twice, but now she won't stop calling and wanting more. That's what I get for cuddling after the deed."

Liam would never prescribe to the number-one rule amongst men: bros before hoes.

When Liam and I were paired up this semester, I was nervous about how Duncan would react to his generally loose morals. But to my surprise, Duncan had said that he preferred Liam over James Hannigan.

James Hannigan and I had briefly dated before Duncan and I had gotten together.

You could say I had a type: brainy, motivated, well-read, and, of course, assholes . . .

Yup. I let James treat me like dirt for two months before Duncan convinced me to dump him. Little did I know at the time that Duncan's role in the demise of that relationship had been selfish. Duncan asked me out on our first date not a week after James and I had called it quits.

Liam was relatively harmless compared to James. When James found out that Duncan and I had started dating, he made it his mission to undermine me at any chance that was presented. During one of the interviews for our mentorship, he sabotaged my stack of talking-point index cards by spilling not one, but two cups of coffee on them. The first cup had drenched my cards, and the second had splashed over the front of my white silk shirt. I'd recovered from losing my notes—I'd memorized them anyway—but he'd started a rumor that I'd only gotten my mentorship because the professor had seen through my wet top.

It was safe to say that I preferred Liam to James as well. Liam was like a dog who hadn't been neutered yet. Energetic, horny, and constantly seeking attention.

Like right now as he flirted openly with the barista who looked like she was regretting whatever life choices that lead her to the opening shift.

I shook my head and took the rare book—that I had at this point stolen—out of my bag to examine one last time before Liam returned with my triple-shot mocha. The feeling of being watched became much more intentional when my fingers slipped between the pages.

Maybe whatever I was looking for was closer than I thought.

"Here you are, partner." He set down my mocha and sat across from me. "You okay? You seem more spacey than usual."

"Just tired. After this paper, I'll be able to sleep better." I gave him a small smile with my half truth.

He was a fuckboy, but he was also attentive. A dangerous combo for any single woman who encountered him.

"As long as that brain of yours doesn't melt before our presentation next Thursday. I'll email you my portion tonight." He took a long sip of his iced coffee then smiled around his straw when I didn't break my stare. "What?"

"Do you believe in demons?"

His brow crinkled. I didn't know why I was asking. I obviously knew the answer. Maybe I needed confirmation from someone else that I hadn't slipped through a glitch in the matrix or been the center of a mean joke gone too far.

"I think we all have our own battles to wage." He delivered his answer like I looked as unstable as I felt. "Are you sure you're okay?"

"I don't mean like mental health, and yes, I'm fine in that department. I take my meds every day along with my contraceptive." I tossed my hair from one side to the other. "What I meant was, do you think there are real physical demons? Like biblical demonic entities that can manifest in solid form on this plane?"

"Was there a *Buffy* marathon on or something last night?" His uncomfortable laugh brought me back to my senses. Of course he would think I was losing it; I was sounding deranged.

"No. *Charmed*. The old version," I lied. "It just got me thinking, with all the old texts and journals we catalog, if what some of these accounts say isn't a little true. These exorcisms have to have some sort of validity to them, right?"

"Science, poor social status, and a hundred other explanations cover why people believed in witches and possessions back then. Schizophrenia wasn't declared a mental illness until 1887, and it has taken almost ninety years to get from its initial discovery to what we know of it now. That alone explains thousands of so-called possessions."

I knew he was right, but I also knew he was wrong. And there was no way I could prove it to him either way.

"Alyssa Milano is so hot though. Solid binge pick." He tapped my hand on the side of my coffee cup and then leaned back in his chair, checking his phone.

I let the conversation die with that admission. Whatever Vassago and I were tangled up in was going to have to continue to be my own dark secret.

CHAPTER 4

VASSAGO

T he seams of the book's holy pages were stained with the blood of both the damned and the innocent. Seeing Celeste's delicate fingertips tenderly examine its contents filled me with rage and longing. What about the object garnered her admiration more than the demon she'd summoned with it?

The book had brought me to her, but that was all it was good for. If it weren't spelled in protection, I would have destroyed it ages ago.

After Celeste tucked the priest's diary away, she chatted with a human man whom she spent too much time with. Any time with any being other than me was a waste, but this one, in particular, looked at her meaningfully when she wasn't paying attention. He knew what to order for her when they dined together and always kept a chair open for her during their classes. He could have gotten away with being an attentive friend if it weren't for the hours he spent picturing her face on the women he fucked or while he pleasured himself.

Outside of the library that evening, Celeste walked to the parking lot and got into her car. She was one of the last humans left on campus. Three vehicles were parked in the lot, and one of them caught my eye: a Ducati Streetfighter with a custom license plate that read *MONEY*.

The last time I'd owned anything made by that automotive engineer, it had been one of the first Scramblers in blue. This brand-new Streetfighter was a blazon red with two thin black lines running from tip to tail.

It had to be mine.

I could have bought one, but it wouldn't have been the same. Whoever owned this bike had the one other thing on this plane that I desired, and who would I be if I didn't act on my nature?

With a wave of my hand, the bike roared to life between my legs and practically purred with a flick of my wrist on the gas. I kicked off and followed Celeste back to her townhouse, which was several miles away. She had a headstart, but with the New York City traffic —and a lot of illegal lane splitting—I caught up to her quickly.

Being Celeste's unseen shadow meant that I could be near her while she was studying or working, and in my spare time, I'd brushed up on pop culture, motor vehicles, and music. The only place I couldn't follow her into was her home. To my frustration, the friend who dabbled in sex-store witchcraft also liked to gift her friends with protective knickknacks. Though she didn't study true magic or practice regularly, her intent for the objects was present. So the angelite crystal hidden in a red charm bag hanging above Celeste's door was strong enough to keep me out without Celeste's explicit desire for me to enter.

I'd learned many things about my gift since she'd released me. Celeste drank too much coffee, slept far too little, and didn't care for anyone's opinions on her life or vices. She was heavily preoccupied with her higher education and the position in the program she had wished for. Her dream was to eventually discover things lost to time. Her thirst for knowledge rivaled that of the men I'd known through the years, scholars who'd wasted away in front of their books, telescopes, and radioactive substances.

I owed her the wildest dreams she had. I would be the pathway to her ultimate goal and the life she wanted to create for herself. It was more than any of the books in her favorite library could give her. Though, in my humble opinion, I was the most interesting thing she could have discovered while flipping through the books of priests and monks.

In the short hours that I allowed her to exist outside of my orbit, I was with my brother, who was as equally off the deep end as I was.

Seere, the Prince of Wrath, had his own engrossment, a human woman by the name of Sloane. The first night I was free, I stepped through the void to his doorstep in Malibu and he'd met me with open arms and an ease that felt like no time had passed.

Being trapped for half a century came with the stress of having to adjust to the current state of the world. While fifty years is only a drop in the bucket when living for an eternity, a lot can happen in the rapidly growing human world. Wars had come and gone. Things had been invented and reinvented, and television shows that had been popular before were now being revitalized as live-action movies with younger faces.

I'd never felt old. The concept didn't exist for me. I never got stuck in my ways because I had to adapt with the times. But the last week of being back among the living had been like stepping into a new dimension.

Seere now owned and operated several establishments around the city. Four of them were real estate, but his favorite was a strip club on a particularly dingy street outside the main drag of Los Angeles. The Red Room was dark, intimate, and otherwise lucrative. Unlike the exclusive dance club and bar that Sitri and the Watcher had developed while I was gone, The Red Room was only for human clients. The dancers, however, were demonic.

Seere had invited me along for the opening shift and was busily stalking the bar as I walked around the main stage. The sound of my borrowed loafers was deadened by the velvet-like carpets that surround the shiny black stage. It was polished to the point that my reflection stared back up at me with tired, baggy eyes and the scowl that had been fixed in place for longer than I could remember.

"You want a drink?" Seere called from across the room. "I'm making one for myself and Semper."

Semper was his bartender for the night, a lesser demon who worked within his legion as a commander. I'd known her for just as long as any other, but now she was covered in tattoos and piercings.

"I'm not staying long. I have to make sure Celeste is at home tonight."

It was Friday night. Celeste—I'd realized this morning—didn't have class on Fridays. She had been home all day doing chores and catching up on things around her home. She'd told her male friend that someone would be returning from a trip on Sunday, and whoever Duncan was, he was worth deep-cleaning her house.

"Are you sure that's a good idea?" He looked up at me through stitched brows. "You've spent all your time watching that human since you've been released."

"What else is worth my time?" I shrugged and pulled myself onto the stool across from him at the bar.

"You're in the new millennium, brother. You can do anything. Be anyone. Travel this newer world and find your place back in the fold. Your throne has sat empty for many years. Lucifer will want to know you're safe."

I cringed at that. Lucifer had been a means to an end. Following him in the Fall was my rebellion against our Father. The years that followed and my reign as Prince of Envy for the deviants of Hell were consolations. I didn't want to return to Heaven like a wounded dog with my tail between my legs, but I'd also never reveled in my position at Lucifer's table. Being a strong and powerful fighter was in my nature—my essence. Every cell that made me whole had been created to be loyal, strong, and a warrior for whatever cause that was put at my feet.

My position as a prince of Hell was nothing but a glamor, a hollow adornment that gave me a higher rank in the hierarchy that I'd helped build.

What I wanted was a purpose.

What I needed was Celeste. To protect her and give her everything she'd ever desired just so she'd sing a damning gospel of my name while I devoured her, body and soul.

The itch under my skin to go to her side blossomed once again. "I have seen every inch of this world countless times. My throne will never truly be empty until the human race fails to exist, and by then, Heaven and Hell will be bursting at their seams. Tonight—and any other night I see fit—my eyes will be focused on Celeste."

"Fine. But once you've gotten your fill, come by before you head home." Seere leaned over the bar, his thick arms holding his muscular frame above the polished surface.

"I will."

CHAPTER 5
CELESTE

I'd been cleaning for days. Duncan was on the train home from Boston and would be back in New York at any moment. He hated it when the house was a mess, and his standards were high since his mother was a professional organizer and party planner. I liked living in a less restricted way, but he had a place for everything and had to have everything in its place.

When the keys unlocked the door almost a half hour earlier than I expected, I practically jumped out of my skin.

"Hey! You're home early." I tried to hide the slight disappointment in my voice when Duncan came in with his suitcase trailing behind him.

"I caught a quick transfer." He took me in and smiled wide, melting the worry I had about the state of the house.

Duncan wrapped his arms around my waist and

lifted me for a quick spin. He was only slightly taller than me but loved to pick me up as if he were some large caveman. My socked feet hit the rug a moment later, and he held my face in his hands for a sweeter-than-expected kiss.

"What was that for?" I giggled.

"I have amazing news for the both of us." He slumped off his backpack and got down on his knees to rummage through it.

I crossed my arms and waited for him to find whatever it was he was looking for. Without thinking, I glanced out of the living room window, and my blood ran cold. Standing on the sidewalk was a tall, dark figure. Though it was night and the streetlight was shining bright over his head, light somehow refracted off of him or was absorbed by the horror he was made from. I knew it was Vassago without a doubt in my mind, and I hadn't prepared myself for the moment I would have to either tell Duncan I summoned a demon or save his life from said possessive demon.

"Celeste." Duncan's voice brought me back to him. "You okay?"

"Yeah, just anxious for you to tell me your good news." I put on a smile but doubted he would notice that it was insincere.

"Here."

The paper he handed me was an acceptance letter to the fellowship program at Boston University's anthropology department. The official letterhead at the top prefaced the invitation with his name scrawled across the first line.

"You applied to Boston's program? When?" I shook my head in disbelief.

"Last month. I wanted to surprise you. We're going to Boston, baby." He balled his fists and excitedly pumped them, then clapped his hands together. "We need to go out and celebrate. Get dressed."

"I am dressed," I said, looking down at my jeans and T-shirt.

"Yeah, but you know what I mean." He pulled me into his body. "Wear that sexy little dress I like and get all dolled up for me."

"Duncan." I pushed him away then rounded the coffee table to put distance between us. "I'm not transferring to BU. Why would you assume I would do that? What about the fellowship? You haven't even heard back from the board yet and you're just bailing on our plans?" The questions started falling out of my mouth louder and louder. "What about my courses? Or our research thesis partners? We can't just up and leave them."

"You're acting really childish and selfish right now."

"Selfish?" I coughed out.

"Yes. You're acting like a total bitch. This is a great opportunity for us both. You're not going to get the fellowship; we both know that. I'm trying to build a future for us, Celeste, and you're always getting in the way with your hyper-independent feminist bullshit."

The pressure of my blood pounding against my

eardrums was building in my head, pushing hot tears to my eyes.

We'd had this fight often. Though we'd met during my last year of the masters program, Duncan always assumed that once we got married, I would become a housewife and mother. He called me the perfect partner for his future genius children.

"I'm not going to Boston." My voice cracked, and the river of tears burned my cheeks.

"I know it's scary." The anger in his voice melted into a calming parental tone. "But you'll do great there. I have a guaranteed spot. We can't pass that up."

"Duncan—"

"I just got home. I'm tired and don't want to fight. Will you please go get dressed so we can celebrate my win?"

I didn't answer.

Instead, I gave him a small smile of defeat and went to our bedroom closet to put on the dress he wanted me to wear and get ready to bite my tongue all evening. There was no use fighting with him until the next day. If I said no, we would be awake for hours, screaming at each other until one of us finally locked ourselves in the bathroom until the other fell asleep on the couch. It was a toxic pattern I'd been stuck in for years.

My eyes strained against the urge to look out the window and search for the most radical solution to the war raging in my chest. I'd asked for the fellowship, but why couldn't I ask for a clean break from my boyfriend?

Because that was cowardly, wrong, and dangerous.

Vassago was a demon, not a fairy godfather. Not only did his help come with strings I hadn't found the end to yet, but he would likely kill Duncan rather than peacefully remove him from my life. And as much of an asshole as he was being, I did love Duncan.

Didn't I?

CHAPTER 6
VASSAGO

I wasn't going to let Celeste out of my sight, especially with that man back in town and under her roof. Another man's hands on my gift was a surefire way for him to meet a premature death. The only reason he was still breathing was that I didn't want to be the cause of Celeste's sadness or pain. But I could sense his stained soul and salivated at the thought of being his eternal punishment when Celeste finally left him for me.

The radiation of their argument clouded them as they got into Celeste's car. Whatever the fight had been about, Celeste was hiding her true feelings for the sake of an evening out. Her face was covered in makeup, but it didn't erase the disappointment from her eyes.

I followed them to the packed nightclub in downtown Manhattan, where Duncan took several shots one after another, hollering between each one like he'd won some sort of lottery. Celeste ordered a vodka cranberry and sipped at it for the first hour as Duncan danced like a fool. He was too immersed in his own ego to notice when she slipped from the crowd to the ladies' room.

The music being pumped through too many speakers followed us down the dark hallway. Her long black hair covered a small tattoo on her shoulder. The thin line work spelled something out, but with the distance I kept between us, I couldn't read it. That was about to change.

My hand flew out to the bathroom door and held it open. Celeste's bulging eyes followed my arm up to my face and all color drained from her cheeks. I took a step into her, my chest backing her into the single-stall bathroom. I flicked the light on then locked the graffiti-covered door.

"What are you doing here?" her thin voice croaked.

"Are you afraid?" Keeping my hands low at my sides, I showed her my empty palms in good faith.

"No." She cleared her throat and rolled her shoulders back. "But you've been hiding from me since I released you. Why are you here now?"

She looked around the filthy room, but only briefly. Her eyes didn't stray far from the beast that had cornered her.

"You were upset."

Her brows furrowed. "What?"

"When that man returned from his trip." I stepped closer, and she didn't back away. "He upset you, didn't he?"

Her lips tightened into a line, and she took a long inhale before answering, "How would you know that?"

I was only inches away. Her eyes had to roll up to meet mine, and the subtle tilt of her chin sent my blood racing. "You're not inconspicuous."

"I'm fine. It was just an argument. I don't need reinforcements from Hell."

I chuckled at that. Deep down, I could see how madly she wanted to flex that muscle. The one that would unleash me onto whomever she saw fit. That sort of power was intoxicating for anyone.

Good.

"It would be so easy, though." I lowered my face close to her ear and whispered, "A snap of your fingers. A snap of his neck."

She shivered. My fingertips lingered at the angles of her hips and lightly suggested she come closer.

"Why are you always hiding?" she breathed as my arm snaked around her back and drew her in. "If you're so obsessed with being close to me, why are you never where I can see you?"

I smiled against the side of her face. "Is that what you think about when he's not around? How badly you want to see me?" I inhaled her sweet perfume and the sweat that had coated her skin. "Do you wonder what would happen if you whispered my name in the cold, empty library?"

Her hands gripped the back of my shirt, her nails dug into my flesh, and my cock swelled in my jeans.

"Does your pussy pulse at the thought of the cold wooden table against your back as I feast on you?"

Her knees buckled, and the weight of her body in my arms drew the last thread of my restraint tight. The heady scent of her heated skin so close to my teeth made my mouth water.

"Do you dream of a dimly lit bathroom that echoes with the sound of you panting my name while a line of people listen with hearts full of jealousy on the other side of the door?"

"Please." Her shallow word brought a groan from deep in my chest.

"You would never have to beg me for anything, Celeste. I could give you anything your heart desires if you allow me to."

Reason emerged in her hazy lucid dream. Something I'd said was too much and burst the seductive fantasy bubble I'd almost trapped her in.

"You're a demon."

"I'm *your* demon," I reminded her.

"In every sense of the word." Her eyes dropped. She wasn't looking at anything in particular, but not holding my gaze meant she wasn't giving in to me tonight.

I hooked her chin with my finger to bring her lips up to mine but did not kiss them—though it took everything in me not to taste what was mine.

"All you have to do is call." I let her body go and seeped back into the shadows between light and dark.

CHAPTER 7
CELESTE

T he splash of cold water on my face did nothing to extinguish the heat that was sourced in my core but spilling from every one of my pores.

Vassago was gone, but I couldn't shake the feeling of his eyes still on me. His arm around me had felt safe and strong. Lethal. I could still smell him on me in faint wisps, and I wanted nothing more than to be wrapped up in his scent like a blanket until it became my own.

Once he pushed me into the bathroom and I realized he was solid, a wall of fear had hit me. Was he there to take me away—or worse, hurt someone? The mixture of emotions that slammed into me when he appeared sent me into momentary shock and disbelief. I'd almost convinced myself that I was obsessing over him like a preteen over a floppy-haired boy band singer because I hadn't been able to stop picturing him. I had been sure that the electricity I felt when he'd touched me that first night had been an over exaggeration.

I was wrong. The empty feeling in my gut was proof of that.

I knew it would be easy to let him take anything he desired from me. That was what scared me the most. I'd never let anyone break through the layers of lead walls I'd created for myself. I'd decided long ago that nothing would get between me and my goals. I'd seen too many of my friends let men derail them, all for someone presenting them with a precious stone and a promise to support them forever.

A lifelong partner was never something I planned for. Dating Duncan staved off the loneliness, and he understood what it was like to be in a competitive program and the dedication I had to our field.

Or so I'd thought.

I was so angry at Duncan for making a choice outside the parameters we'd established on a whim.

If Duncan wanted to leave Columbia University, then he was welcome to do so. Parting ways so we could pursue our individual goals was perfectly logical.

What had been eating at me the most was the unde-niable sentiment that his dreams were more important than mine and that I should value his career over my own.

There was a difference between knowing what was best for me—and ultimately for Duncan—and actually going through with it.

I didn't want to argue with him while he was drunk,

but my mind was set. I was going to break things off with Duncan . . . without demonic interference.

I glanced around the dimly lit bathroom one more time then headed back to the dance floor. Duncan was exactly where I left him. Except instead of dancing in a group of other drunk college students, he had found some girl. Her ass was grinding on his crotch while his hands traveled over her hips, thighs, and stomach. He wasn't groping her, but he was acting as if he hadn't been driven here by his girlfriend.

I contemplated leaving him there to find his own way home then decided against it. I walked up behind him and tapped him on the shoulder. His head whipped around, and his glassy eyes tried—and failed—to focus on mine.

"There you are, baby!" His genuine surprise caused the woman he was dancing with to turn in his hold and give me a sour look. "This is Erin. She loves to dance and goes to school at NYU."

"Did you get her zodiac sign, too?" I looked between them, sarcasm tipping my tongue and scrunching my nose.

"I'm a Capricorn," Erin stated matter-of-factly.

"And I'm a bitch. Time to go, Duncan." I cupped the back of his arm and pulled him away.

"Thanks for the dance," he called back to her, then he followed me out to my car.

"Y̶ou were jealous." Duncan's head rolled against the headrest to face me. "It was hot."

"I wasn't jealous of that random woman. I'm annoyed that you're so drunk that you forgot who you came with." I knew explaining was useless; he wouldn't remember in the morning.

"I couldn't forget who I came with," he slurred. "You're the hottest bitch alive."

"How many drinks did you end up having tonight? You were only on number four when I went to the bathroom."

"I had a few shots with her before we started dancing." He wiggled his ass in his seat. "She was a great dancer. How come you never dance with your ass on me?"

He reached his hand across the divide and pushed my dress up. I gave him a smack on his wrist, but he clamped his fingers on my thigh.

"Don't be like that, baby. I know what you like."

"We're almost home. Then we can get you to bed."

I pried his grip off of me and forced his hand onto his own lap with a demeaning pat to his knuckles.

"You're trying to get me into bed, huh? Sexy little whore for me?"

I rolled my eyes. He only ever used dirty talk when he

was intoxicated, and it made my skin crawl. The thought of him sweating on top of me as he flopped around like a beached whale with his dick out pushed bile up my throat. He was terrible in bed when he was drunk.

Something tingled at my hips, and my mind went back to Vassago's light touch. The gentle pressure had forced me to cut off all other sensations in order to feel the tips of his fingers on my body. Warm musk and sweet fig wafted over me again, and I wondered if he was close by.

He wasn't in the car, right?

I looked into the rearview mirror and let out a relieved breath.

Duncan was close to passing out, and a kernel of embarrassment settled in my stomach. I didn't think I would have been able to stand Vassago seeing the man I'd been committed to slumped in his seat after pawing at me.

Why would it matter? Nothing could happen between me and a literal Hell monster. Whatever Vassago's intentions were, they were not to fulfill every fantasy I had about him fucking me senseless in every corner of the library. Or in every room of my house.

My skin heated again at the scenario playing in my mind. Vassago's hands forcing my legs apart as I drove, his fingers plunging inside of me, all the while telling me which way to turn. I could almost hear him say, "Only two more turns, then you can come all over my fingers."

A loud blare of a horn snapped me back to reality, and I straightened the wheels back into my own lane.

Duncan shook awake. "What happened?" He looked around, more sober than moments before.

"There was an animal in the road," I lied and pulled at the hem of my dress, noticing how damp my inner thighs were.

Duncan slumped over the center console and gripped my knee. "You're burning up, baby."

I turned the air conditioner on full blast. The fever of my own making wasn't going to be the reason I crashed my car.

"One more turn," I said mostly to myself.

I needed to get out of the car and into an ice-cold shower.

If just the idea of Vassago's hands on my body had turned me into a molten puddle, what would happen if I actually let him have his way with me?

The nose of the vehicle lit the driveway of our townhouse, and as soon as I cut off the engine, I was popping out of the driver's seat and heading to unlock the front door. I thought I would have to haul Duncan into the house, but to my surprise, he was right behind me, his acidic breath at my neck.

"I can't wait to get you naked, baby. Give you the time of your life."

"Doubtful," I said, probably too loud.

Once inside, I made my way to the bathroom with Duncan on my heels. "You're so eager for me."

"I need to shower. Wait for me in our room." I tried

to shut the door, but he'd already wedged himself inside.

"Have to pee."

I rolled my eyes and turned on the shower while he used the toilet. My skin was on fire, and if I didn't cool down soon, I was going to explode.

The ailment was in my head, but so was Vassago. Wasn't he?

I stripped off my dress and my shoes as fast as I could without giving Duncan the satisfaction of seeing me bare, then I stepped into the water and sucked in a haggard breath. The freezing spray hit my face and brought the sting of makeup and sweat to my eyes, but it dulled the ache between my legs.

Lathering my loofa and lost in thought, I washed the smell of the bar off my skin and the stain of hands from my body. Vassago and Duncan had touched me, and one of them was causing me to overheat.

"Someone's at the door," Duncan called from somewhere in the house.

My stomach sank.

I knew who it was. I could feel it in my bones. Had I thought about him too much? Did I somehow internally call out to him with all the depraved urges my body craved?

CHAPTER 8
VASSAGO

I watched them enter the house.

Celeste had a new irritation and—selfishly—I knew it was because of me. It didn't take much of my influence to fluster my darling gift. A sleight of my invisible hand from the backseat of her car and her body reacted like I knew it would.

Though I'd promised myself that I would only ensure she made it home safely, I couldn't suppress the urge to make my presence known to Duncan.

When I knocked on the door, there was a crash and then a yell from the man I was restraining myself from killing just for sport. He answered in only his T-shirt and underwear.

My blood turned to fire.

"Who are you?" His words slurred together in an amalgamation of distrust and drunken cockiness.

"Where is Celeste?" I strained against the rage this human was building inside of me.

"Who the fuck are you, dude?"

"Where is she?" Having to repeat myself was only going to earn him my fury, but before I could introduce him to my fists, Celeste came running to the door in a towel.

"What are you doing here?" Her frantic voice snapped me from the seething fool I was being.

"I was checking that you got home safely from the bar—"

"The bar?" Duncan's irate face fixed on Celeste. "Is that why you disappeared for so long? You were messing around with this"—he looked me up and down—"asshole?"

I knew who was a more desirable specimen of manhood in the eyes of women—but more importantly in Celeste's. Duncan was weak in many aspects, including potency. Aside from being a feeble human, he didn't compare to Celeste in intelligence or resilience.

"Duncan," Celeste warned him, but he was too stubborn to listen, "Just wait for me in our room."

"Fuck that," he spat. "I knew something was going on when you weren't excited about Boston. It's because you're cheating on me with this gym bro."

"I'm not cheating on you. Stop. Please just let me explain."

Duncan crossed his arms and squared his shoulders. "Explain it to me then. Who is this guy? How does he know where we live?"

"I-I . . ." Celeste looked between Duncan and me until finally giving up.

I smirked and leaned against the doorframe.

"Please, Vass, just leave," she pleaded, but it lacked force.

"Tell me you're fine and don't need me to stay and I will go."

Duncan stepped between us. "She's fine, you dick. And she's taken, so fuck off or I'll give you a lesson on sniffing around where you don't belong."

"I know exactly where I belong." I let my eyes travel down Celeste's dripping body.

"Vass."

This time, Celeste pleaded, and I knew I was pushing her too far.

"I'm only a call away." I flicked my eyes up to the small red charm bag hanging above the threshold of her door.

Her eyes followed mine, and understanding dawned. In that brief moment, I wondered how many nights she'd been waiting for me to appear at her bedside.

Duncan snatched the protective spell and tossed it into the bushes that lined the driveway. He'd just done me a favor and had written his own death warrant. "I knew Callie didn't give you that witchy crap. It was from this weirdo, wasn't it?" His noxious attitude intensified the longer Celeste remained coolheaded.

"Duncan, you need to calm down. I'll tell you everything tomorrow morning when you're sober. Vass is just a friend who is leaving now." She waved me off, but I wasn't going to move. Not until I did the damage I'd decided needed to be done.

There was an electrified flash of anger and jealousy in Duncan's expression as he looked between Celeste and me. He was easily manipulated by my influence, and the dark smile on my face only drew him closer to madness. Devious images of my mouth on her neck and my rock-hard body lying on top of hers as she moaned my name filled his imagination, placed there by my metaphorical hand.

Celeste raked her fingers through her damp hair, and the top of her towel slumped slightly, giving me the most mouthwatering view of the swell of her plump breasts. I dropped my chin and wet my lips, a show all for Duncan, but my sweet gift blushed at the attention.

"You motherfucker!" Duncan's fist came flying, but his drunken attempt at violence was no match for my demonic speed.

I batted his arm away, and he fell against the door.

"Fucking dick," Duncan gritted out.

"That's enough!" Celeste yelled, pushing Duncan into the living room and giving me one last look before shutting the door on me.

CHAPTER 9

CELESTE

I couldn't believe he'd shown himself to Duncan. Aside from my disbelief, I was in shock from the whole encounter. The challenge on Vassago's face was intoxicating, but the hunger in his eyes when they landed on me had my skin on fire once again.

He was going to be the death of me.

Duncan stumbled back to his feet and looked around as if he were going to find the six-foot-two "gym bro" waiting to take a swing at him. When he realized the door had shut, his focus zeroed in on me.

"You fucking bitch," he seethed. A dangerous red anger bloomed on his face. "First, you don't want to come to Boston, and now you have strange men showing up to our house in the middle of the night? How long has this been going on?"

He was no longer slurring his words. Stony sobriety had found him, and he was ready to go for several rounds. Tears welled on my lashes, and I held my towel tight around my shaking body. I didn't dare look out the window, but I could feel Vassago watching me from his nightly post. Would the demon come to my defense after inciting the scene playing out?

"Answer me!" Duncan shouted with his fists in his hair.

"I just met him. I don't know how he knew where we lived, and he's never been in the house," I answered honestly. "He is not the reason I don't want to go to Boston. My life is here in New York. You know that."

I inched closer to him and placed a tentative hand on his shoulder. He didn't recoil, but his head snapped up, and the wild look in his gaze made my blood run cold.

"Your life is with me, Celeste." The hard lines on his face melted before he took me into his arms. "We need each other, right?"

I nodded against his sweat-damp shirt, trying my best to hold back the tears and screams caught in my chest. "That's right."

He softened around me, his Hyde receding and giving way to Jekyll to lull me back into his web before—

"And I know nothing happened between you and that guy. We both know that if he knew what a lousy lay you are, he wouldn't bother."

He struck exactly where he'd aimed.

My eyes burned and leaked. My tears mixed with the perspiration his pores had wept during his overreaction, and I was now being punished for both.

"Let's go to sleep." He rubbed his hand up and down my bare arm before letting go.

"I'll be right in." I sniffed.

I locked the front door and spun around to press my back to the cool wood. If it weren't for the class I had in only five hours, I wouldn't follow Duncan. The idea of sleeping next to him felt like going to bed with a serial killer. His hands were covered in the blood of my self-esteem and the future he'd strangled out of me.

Sleeping on the couch would only cause a prolonged argument in the light of day, so I mustered the last bit of strength I had for the night and went to our room. My stomach was in knots, but I'd stopped crying. I slipped on my night shirt and got into the sheets next to Duncan, who was scrolling on his phone. The light illuminated his blank face and cast a blue hue to his blond hair.

I plugged my own device in and laid it screen-side down on my nightstand. I didn't need a random notification lighting the room with tension still coursing through the air.

Duncan rolled over and scooped an arm around me, apparently done looking at whatever he'd been going through. His other hand moved my hair off my neck. It had mostly dried but was still moist, and I didn't have it in me to blow-dry it. He pressed his lips to my neck, and bile threatened my throat.

"You smell so good." His tongue flicked over my skin. "You taste even better. Fuck, I missed you."

His hard-on pressed into my lower back, and I realized that he had taken off his clothes before getting into bed.

"You're so passionate when we fight. Such a sexy, stubborn mouth you have, Celeste."

I flinched as his hand at my belly moved down between my legs. His dick nudged at my entrance.

"Duncan. Not tonight. Please. I have to get up for class soon and just need some sleep." I tried to scoot out of his hold.

His arm banded hard around me and pulled me under him. I was on my stomach in an instant with his groin flush to my ass. He'd been semi-hard a moment ago, but the thrill of taking what he wanted had gotten him to full mast.

"Don't be like that, baby. I know what you like."

He didn't.

"You love it when I beg."

I didn't.

"Tomorrow night, okay?" I pushed myself up on my elbows and looked behind me.

He groaned in frustration and flopped back onto his spot like a petulant child who had been told he wasn't getting a new toy.

"Fine, but you owe me a blow job before you leave for class." He pouted, rolled over, and was snoring within minutes.

I would be long gone before he woke up. My class was hours before his, and he valued sleep more than getting his dick wet from a "lousy lay."

That little comment would be forever seared in my

brain. I tucked it away with all the other small, back-handed things he'd said to me in the past. Like the time he met my parents and said he hoped I didn't look like my mother when I was her age because he'd have to trade me in for a younger model. He'd said this at the party I'd thrown for her after her last round of chemotherapy. It was the reddest flag, but we'd just moved into the townhouse and I'd had nowhere else to go.

I pulled the blankets under my chin, and my thoughts traveled once more to the demon I felt lurking outside. The warm feeling of safety tipped my fingers and toes until I fell into dreams where a dark figure's hands brought me to my breaking point over and over.

CHAPTER 10
VASSAGO

C eleste had slammed the door in my face. She'd chosen Duncan over me, and I was willing to do anything to see his bones ground to paste. But the heartbroken look she'd given him was the crack in the armor I needed to shatter her whole guard.

With the envy I'd inspired, I'd imbued doubt within both of them. Though, I knew I was only adding fuel to a fire lit long before I'd arrived. Where Duncan's rage felt like a freshly lit match that struck and sizzled in the moment with high intensity, Celeste's felt like a flow of a volcano at a constant sputter.

I could say I achieved two victories in the altercation: getting under Duncan's skin and into the recesses of his mind and the spelled barricade was broken. The ward on her home was gone, which meant I could enter when I wanted, but not tonight. She needed her sleep and I was due for a drink with my brother.

The next few days, I watched Celeste from afar. Her classes were long, but her study hours were longer. I hid within the shadows during those late sessions in the library and watched as she drank too much coffee and didn't eat nearly enough.

She was mine to care for, after all. And when the day came that she finally gave over to me, I would ensure that all her needs were met. For now, slipping an extra snack into her bag or refilling her water bottle while her back was turned were my only contributions without directly interfering.

She and Duncan had been on minimal speaking terms since I'd intercepted their reunion celebration, due in part to Duncan frantically setting his transfer in motion. From over her shoulder, I read several text reminders from him telling her to see her guidance counselor and to get a copy of her transcripts. She ignored them, and pride expanded my chest. She was a fighter, and she wasn't going to be pushed into someone else's version of her.

I'd stayed close, gently waking her when she fell asleep with her head in her books.

I revved the engine of my motorcycle at stoplights that she sat at far too long.

I only left her vicinity when I saw the small light of her phone die out for the night through her window.

She could ignore me for now, but sooner or later, she would say my name and bring me to her side.

Until then, I was her guardian, my clipped wings laid at her feet as a proposition.

(PLEASE TAKE A MOMENT TO REVISIT THE CONTENT WARNING PAGE AND THE SYNOPSIS LINK.)

CHAPTER II
CELESTE

riday finally came. Duncan was headed back to Boston the next morning to secure an apartment on campus to finish out the rest of the semester. I'd convinced him that I would join him during his summer internship, but I had no real intention behind the promise.

Vassago had been a constant visitor in my dreams, and in the waking hours, I felt him within arm's reach everywhere I went. I noticed the motorcycle he'd been riding and was curious how he'd gotten it, but I figured it was better if I left that can of worms firmly tinned.

He'd been loitering on campus in solid form more often. I wasn't sure if he knew that I was also keeping tabs on him, but it was hard to ignore the looks he would get from other women as they passed him.

As I sat in one of the coffee shops on campus on Thursday, he was forced to be my sentinel in his human form because of the western facing windows that chased shadows from the well-lit cafe. His eyes rarely detached themselves from me, which meant I was the one of us privy to the line of women giggling with their companions at the gorgeous man sipping a black coffee with two sugars.

"Did you see him? I wonder if he's the new adjunct professor for the literature department," a cute blonde said to her friend. "I bet he's a master at linguistics."

"Sign me up. I could use that kind of motivation to go to class," her friend added before they found a seat positioned in his direct line of sight.

I smiled to myself.

His type of attention was obsessive and classically dangerous, but with his intense, dark eyes only shining for me, I could let my ego have the win. Anyone who saw him dropped their jaw, but I knew that only I existed in his world.

The rev of the flashy motorcycle behind me signaled that I'd made it home safely. He'd be close by until I turned the lights off. His routine was more predictable than my own at this point.

I parked my car in my driveway and pulled my messenger bag onto my shoulder. Out of the corner of my eye, I saw the tall figure remove his helmet. He'd parked across the street again, this time not bothering to avoid the streetlight overhead. His gaze on my back felt hot, and I paused for too long, wondering if I should say something. Bid him goodnight?

With a calming breath, I shut the car door and walked to the edge of the driveway. The short distance felt like miles, but in the blink of an eye, he was standing over me.

"You don't have to stay. Wherever you go after I go to bed—you can go there now." I wasn't sure what my point was, but I felt guilty for leading him on.

He peered down at me, his eyes as black as the night above us. "Or I could stay." The low timbre of his voice rippled into my body, and I ached to agree.

"I don't know why you would."

His lips twisted into a crooked smile. "To protect my gift."

"Why do you call me that?"

"Because you are mine. A gift to be treasured for the rest of my eternity."

I shifted from one awkward foot to the other. "You've been guarding me."

There wasn't much room between our bodies, but the electricity I felt raging in that space could have started a fire.

His hand trailed up my arm, then his fingers brushed over my chin and his face dipped close to mine. "I could do a better job of it if you let me into your home."

"You can't come in?"

Was I really asking a demon why he couldn't break into my house?

"I could. But I'd prefer it if you invited me."

"Oh."

His lips widened to a bright, telling smile. A panty-drenching smile that came with heavy eyelids and a posture that was too easy to melt into, like I belonged glued to his side.

"I'll think about it." And I would. For hours and days. "But for now, you should go. I'm headed to bed. I have to take Duncan to the train tomorrow morning."

He raised his head and looked behind me. The muscles in his chest looked both soft and firm. I wondered if there was some sort of gym for only supernatural beings and, if so, when he had the time to go when he spent most of his day watching over me. My hand itched to reach out and feel his broad frame expand as he drew in another breath.

After staring too long, I cleared my throat, bringing his attention back to me.

"If you do change your mind, here." He fished a round object out of the front pocket of his jeans. "Hold it tight and speak my true name. I'll come."

I had no doubt.

The cold metal disk warmed in my fingers quickly, as if it recognized me. Its dull surface was etched with the same boxy beetle I'd seen on the planchette. When I looked up to give him some sort of gratitude, he was gone. So was the motorcycle. He hadn't ridden it away, so I knew he'd left for the night.

A knot in my chest ached at his sudden absence. Maybe I had expected him to stay. I should have felt relieved. Duncan would be on edge with his trip coming up, and the devilishly handsome stalker lurking outside every night had been nagging at him.

Duncan had said numerous times that he didn't

believe in long-distance relationships, so I hoped that I could encourage the distance long enough that our relationship fizzled out for good. I just had to make it through one more night without a big blowup argument. Vassago not being outside the window would make that more obtainable.

"Celeste." Duncan's voice came from the top of the steps.

My head whipped around.

"Hurry up and get inside." He held the door open.

"Okay." I tucked the coin into my pocket and did what he asked.

My heart slammed against my sternum. Had he seen me talking to Vassago? Seen the demon disappear into the thin night air?

I scurried up the stairs into the entryway. When I turned around to face Duncan with half-hearted explanations, he was slamming the door and turning on me. His hand reached out to grab the scruff of my neck. I yelped as the hair tangled in his fist sent sharp pains shooting through my body.

"Why was he here again?" he seethed through gritted teeth.

"I don't know." I squirmed in his hold. "You're hurting me."

He ignored my plea and pulled me closer. "I see the way you look at him when you think I'm not watching. You look for him everywhere you go and never tell him to leave."

"I told him to leave. He's gone." I tried to keep my

voice level through the searing pain at my scalp. "Please. You're scaring me."

"You haven't touched me since I got back from Boston. Even when you're home, you're not really here. You're only ever with him."

My heart raced and tears blurred my vision, but I could still see the malice on Duncan's face.

I'd never seen him so furious.

He walked us into our bedroom, my shoulder bumping hard against the corner of the doorframe. The backs of my knees hit the mattress, but instead of letting go of me, Duncan pulled me up harder against him. He took my bag off my shoulder and tossed it to the ground.

"You're going to remember whose girlfriend you are. Who fucking owns you." He fisted the top of my blouse and ripped down.

Buttons went flying.

My fingernails clawed into the soft flesh of his arm, but if he felt the pain, he wasn't showing it. "Please don't. Stop. Please!"

His determined fingers pulled at the zipper of my jeans, and when he couldn't get them loose, he threw me onto the bed. My arm hit something hard. The mystery object and I bounced with the force of my landing, but he was quickly on top of me, straddling my thighs. Between my shock and panic, he'd gotten my pants down around my knees.

"Stop!" I cried out again. "No."

"Shut up. You fucking cheating bitch."

His hand flew over my mouth and nose, restricting my breathing. I swung my fists, hoping to connect with his face. He grabbed at the solid mass next to me then brought it up for me to see. It was a metal bar with handcuffs attached to it.

My eyes bulged as his free hand clicked the first cuff to my flailing wrist. The cold metal bit into my skin. He brought the bar down to my throat and put his weight on it as he quickly fastened the other cuff around my other wrist.

I twisted under him and brought the bar up with as much energy as I could muster, but his hand caught the middle before it reached his face. He pulled his shirt off and stuffed the sweaty fabric into my mouth to muffle my screams for help.

"Your stalker fuck buddy can't hear you."

He kicked at my pants, trapping my ankles together, and hooked an arm under my thighs to push his knees between them. The bow of my legs framed his unyielding hips. I bucked, tried to toss my weight from one side to the other to dislodge him, but he held firm. His other hand reached up and pinned the bar to the bed, his dead eyes eating up my vision.

"Do you beg like this for him?"

Hot, grating breath rushed over my cheek. I screamed through my gag and shook my head, trying desperately to convince him that I had remained faithful. If reason hadn't left me at the front door, I would have known that no amount of begging was going to stop him from what he had planned. And he had planned it.

We were not into kink. This bar was brand new. We'd never discussed permissions or hard limits because this would have been one of mine.

"If you're going to be a slut, I'm going to treat you like one."

He pulled my underwear aside before painfully forcing his way inside.

I kicked my feet, shifted my body this way and that, trying to wriggle away, but he laid his full weight on top of me, his hips erratically thrusting. He grunted, snorted, and cursed all while I cried, begged, and thrashed.

When I thought I'd finally angled my pelvis in a way that allowed me to push him away and close my legs, he'd gotten to his feet and pulled me to the edge of the bed. He raised his hand and smacked the top of my thigh.

Shocked and in pain, I twisted away, but it was what he'd wanted. He flipped me on my stomach, exposing my backside to him. The bar—now trapped below my hips—dug into my skin and pulled at my wrists. I looked around the room for anything to distract him, but it was too dark to waiver my options.

Duncan had gone quiet for what felt like too long, but when his hand clamped onto my shoulder, I understood why.

He'd retrieved his phone.

The small, bright light aided him in recording. He

brought the camera lens to my face, the blinding beam only inches away.

"The next time I see that asshole, I'm going to show him how you deserve to get fucked."

The camera moved, and a hard smack landed on my ass. Then another. I screamed and choked on the saliva-soaked T-shirt that jammed itself in the back of my throat.

"That's right, baby, scream for me," he mocked, sticking his dick back into me. "Fight for it."

My heart faltered.

The man raping me had been sleeping next to me for almost two years. This monster had been lurking under the mild-mannered Duncan for as long as I'd known him. I'd never caught the smallest glimpse.

Had he done this before?

It seemed like it. In fact, it felt like every thrust was being savored. Like someone who had been dieting for years indulging in their favorites for the first time in too long.

I hated him. I hated that my body was quenching his disgusting thirst and that I would never be the same after because of him.

If he wanted to see me fight, he would.

But not now.

I forced my body to go limp. His brutal betrayal persisted, but I refused to give him the satisfaction of being his victim. I closed my eyes and waited for him to finish. When he did, his sweaty body collapsed on mine.

"I'm sorry I had to punish you like that, but it drives

me crazy when someone else looks at you." He forced me to face him with a rough pull of my chin. "I know you're sorry and you'll never cheat on me again. I forgive you, Celeste."

The emotions behind his words were hollow, and even worse, he was trying to blame me for his actions. Perhaps in the past, I would have believed him, but it was too late and he'd gone too far.

He moved off of me. "I'm going to bed. We have to get up early for my train."

I choked on one last sob as he loosened the restraints.

"Go clean yourself. You look pathetic."

CHAPTER 12

VASSAGO

O f all my brothers, the one I least expected to find at The Red Room was Gaap, the Prince of Sloth. He and Seere were holed up in the back office when I returned. It was still early on this coast, but the dancers were entertaining a room full of patrons on the other side of the wall.

"There he is," Seere announced as I stepped through the door. "Guess who has some interesting information for you regarding that book you were trapped in."

Gaap opened his arms wide and embraced me, and I returned the adoration with a tight squeeze. He was covered in tattoos and his clothing reminded me of the punk rock movement that had been taking hold before I'd been banished. It suited him.

"You were missed," Gaap said, pulling away and clapping my shoulder.

"From what I understand, you have also recently made your reentrance into the fold."

I perked a brow at the cheeky smile he gave me. "My hand was forced. A crazed priest from the Order by the name of Alessio hunted me for months. Nearly got to me, too, if it weren't for a woman."

Seere propped his feet up on the edge of his desk and linked his fingers behind his neck, obviously pleased with the coincidences between my and Gaap's worlds at the moment.

I crossed my arms and watched Gaap and Seere exchange a look. "I suppose you're here to convince me that duty and our rankings are more important than the humans we owe our lives to?"

"No," Gaap answered.

My chest deflated with the pent-up energy I'd been gathering. "No?" I confirmed.

"Celeste is more important than anything else on this or any other plane. Fight to keep her." Gaap smiled and touched the freshly tattooed black band around his ring finger. Looking closer, the word Pru broke up the thick line.

I felt closer to Gaap than I ever had in the time we'd existed alongside each other. Even in the Fall, our battles didn't coincide. Seere led the legions with me, and through that bond, I was convinced to take a seat at Lucifer's table. Sitri had a soft spot for Gaap, but more often than not, the Prince of Sloth was seen as a rebellious deserter who disappeared for long periods of time through history to fuck his way through entire empires then came back when his money was spent and his life was in shambles.

He resembled a spoiled child on his shallowest level, but in this moment, he understood me.

"Thank you." We exchanged a nod of understanding, and I continued, "What do you know about the book?"

Seere was the one to start. "It's part of a set owned by the priests of the Order of Exorcists. Each member of the brotherhood seems to have their own book that they use to banish demons back to Hell or hide artifacts they deem too dangerous for the public."

That explained the many items Celeste spent hours researching since releasing me.

"They're spelled to keep the unholy out—or in your case, trapped inside." Gaap moved to the corner of the desk and sat with his arms crossed.

"What happens when the priests succumb to time?" I asked them.

"The books are usually passed on to the next generation, who then take up lives dedicated to hunting demons. But we aren't sure what happened to the man who imprisoned you." Seere's frustration laced his words.

I remembered the night I was captured. It had haunted my every waking moment for the first few years of my imprisonment. I'd been in Copenhagen in 1972 at a celebration for the newly crowned Queen of Denmark. The highest in European society had been in attendance, and I'd been accompanied by a young duchess whom I'd become cozy with. After many drinks and a few experimental drugs, we'd found ourselves in an empty council room. One moment, I had the duchess's legs over my shoulders, my face in her cunt, and the next, I was being drawn into darkness.

"The priest who trapped you disappeared several years ago." Seere's somber voice held unwarranted guilt. "From what we've been able to piece together, there isn't confirmation from either side about his fate. He came to the States in the early nineties, but the trail runs cold there."

There was no way my brothers would have been able to locate me. The book hadn't been removed from the shelves at Columbia University in decades. This only confirmed that Celeste had been meant to find it—and to release me.

How many humans had wandered the shelves but never heard my cries for help?

No. I had been delivered to her. The smallest bones in her body had vibrated when she crossed my path.

"You said Alessio had his own book," I said. "Where is it now?"

Anger wrinkled Gaap's face before he responded, "The snake survived, but his book of curses is in the hands of Eligos. We both know how steep the price is for his favors."

"You let the priest live?" I asked.

"I was close to the truest death I'd ever felt. He was wounded, but I wasn't the one who inflicted it." Gaap held up his left hand, showing me the permanent ring on his finger. "Pru. Bravest human I've ever met."

"And you don't know where he is now?"

Seere answered, "Sitri suspects that Alessio is hiding out but has ultimately retreated to his brotherhood. There haven't been rumors of a mounting attack yet, but I wouldn't doubt it's coming. Which leads me to a great favor I must ask of you and your Celeste."

"You want her book," I guessed.

My gaze went to Gaap. "If we have one of our own to decipher without Eli's strings attached, we might have a chance at beating them at their own game."

"This isn't our fight." I wouldn't put Celeste in danger. Ours was a story that had been written far before modern religion or churches were punishing those it saw as sinful.

"If she's with you, she is part of their war." Seere's dark voice rang true, but the itch in my throat begged for me to argue.

I knew he was right.

The Order of Exorcists wouldn't care that I had gladly abandoned my throne in Hell for my gift. They would see her as a sympathizer and kill her on sight.

"Fine." I was defeated but cornered. I hadn't walked through damnation only to find my reason for existing, just for her to be taken from me by radicalized priests. "I will get you the book, but in exchange, you must do something for me."

I gave them the list of names that were competing for a spot in the fellowship that Celeste deserved to have. All but one. James Hannigan was mine. He'd made a show of humiliating Celeste in the classes they shared, and I wanted to watch him beg for her forgiveness.

Seere's ruthless eyes filled with hunger for an opportunity to sink his teeth into someone.

"Consider it done," Gaap said as his farewell before he stepped through the void. I'd sensed his initial hesitation, but I knew he would deliver.

"Thank you, Seere," I said.

"There is no need to say such meaningful words. She's not only important to you, but she's going to be put in more danger than she realizes. You've been her shadow up until now, but soon, you'll have to be her guard dog."

His realization was nothing I wasn't already prepared for. I didn't need more reasons to latch my existence to Celeste's. She was mine. My most precious gift. My soul would have to be sent into oblivion for it to leave hers. And even then, I would claw my way across space and time to return to her.

"Are you headed home for the night?" Seere asked.

A tingle in my chest twisted my lips into a smile and told me my next destination. "Don't wait up."

CHAPTER 13
CELESTE

The tile of the bathroom floor bit into my still-bare bottom as I clutched the small coin Vassago gave me.

Duncan, I was sure, had fallen asleep hours ago, but I couldn't make my arms or legs move from the spot I had sunk to.

I was driving myself insane by asking the same questions over and over, but the same answers came each time.

How could he have done that to me?

Because he was a monster. A rapist.

Why me?

Because I was in his path.

How could I let him do that to me?

I didn't. He gave me no choice.

Another gush of burning tears ran down my cheeks. I'd been trying to work up the nerve either to leave or call Vassago.

Both options felt too hard.

My throat was raw from screaming then vomiting. The skin between my thighs was red and irritated from scrubbing the evidence off me.

I looked down at the coin again. It was so simple, battered and crudely carved with his sigil. It felt as if the most valuable part of it was connected to him.

I heard a rumble from the bedroom. Not footsteps or even a call for me, but I held my breath nonetheless. After a few minutes of silence, I shut my eyes and pressed the warm token to my lips.

At first, I only allowed myself to silently move my lips. Then, I stretched out the first letter, then the second and third until I breathed the last. The air thickened and then fullness surrounded me.

His hand cupped my face. "Open your eyes."

I shook my head.

"Celeste." The sound of his hitched voice saying my name delved deep into a part of my soul that called back in ways I knew it shouldn't.

I lifted my chin and pried my eyelids open. Fury, vitriol, rage, and understanding stared back at me.

"What did he do to you?"

I pursed my lips then let out a ragged sob. "He . . ."

I couldn't say it out loud. I couldn't form the words to express what he'd done. Because it wasn't just the physical violence he'd committed, but what he'd been doing for years. He'd never been interested in foreplay. Didn't care if I ever had an orgasm unless it was a special occasion. He'd built our relationship from the ground up to be all about his needs and pleasures. Duncan had been working up to violence, but he'd been forcing himself on me from day one.

"I'll deal with him later." Vassago pulled me into his lap.

I wrapped my arms around his neck and let my body relax into his. There was a strong sensation of something pulling at the air around us, then darkness. He snapped his fingers, and a light clicked on somewhere in the new space.

I knew we'd gone somewhere because we were no longer sitting on the hard tile of my cramped bathroom. We'd been transported to a spacious but cozy bedroom with warm, forest-green wallpaper. A bed in the corner wasn't made fully, and Vass' leather jacket was tossed haphazardly on the black linen duvet.

"Where are we?"

He held me close to his chest. Sweet fig and spice, I realized, was settled into his bedroom, not just on his skin.

"My brother's home in Malibu, California." He walked us across the room toward one of the only pieces of furniture, a dresser.

"You took me to the other side of the country?"

I watched his face as he lowered me from his hold and my toes pushed into the plush carpet. He kept one arm firmly around my waist as he rummaged through a chest of drawers.

"I brought you somewhere safe. What safer place is there than a house that two princes of Hell live in?"

"P-princes?" My stomach churned.

"Here, they may be a bit big on you, but I'll bring you back a change of clothes in the morning." His voice was soothing but firm, but the crease in his brow had my stomach squirming.

I took the pair of sweatpants he was offering and held them up to my hips. I wasn't scrawny, but he was tall and his hips were wider than mine.

"I . . ." My face heated and my eyes filled with tears again. "I need to shower."

Vassago pulled me into him once again. The muscles in his arms and torso tensed for only a moment. His heavy breath in my hair felt like relief. I fought against the urge to fall apart again.

"I'll get you a towel." He made to move away, but my hand clutched the side of his T-shirt. I didn't want him to leave me, even to walk down the hall.

"I needed you." I looked up into his eyes and saw the regret there. "And you came. Thank you."

"I shouldn't—"

"Don't." I stopped the apology I knew he was about to give. "Even you couldn't have known what Duncan was capable of."

He wrapped an arm around my shoulders and led me down the long hall to a linen closet. The rest of the house was dark except for one room at what seemed to be the top of the stairs. If there was someone else in the house, they were busy. Or at least I hoped they were since all I was wearing was a pair of soiled underwear, a ripped blouse, and my bra.

"The house is beautiful. From what I can see of it."

He turned around, two large fluffy towels in hand. "I'll give you a proper tour tomorrow."

"When are you going to take me home?"

The lines of his face deepened. "Let's talk about that after you're comfortable."

I nodded.

He held my hand and led me back to the bedroom we'd landed in, then into the en suite bathroom.

My nerves were shot, and my head was pounding. Aside from a shower, I needed sleep.

Where *was* I going to sleep?

Vassago started the shower as I looked behind us to the king-sized bed. Several thoughts ran through my mind: How long had he been staying here? And with who? Who was the other prince of Hell? Had anyone else ever slept with him in that bed?

"I'm going to get you a T-shirt then leave you to wash up." He paused but finished his thought quickly when I sucked in a worried breath. "But I won't be far away."

"Okay." I let my shoulders relax and watched his back disappear around the corner.

I set down the pair of sweatpants I'd been holding onto for dear life and pulled my arm out of my torn blouse. It had been one of my favorites. White with blue and purple flowers. It had fit me loosely, which meant I could tie it at the front or tuck it into a skirt. Now, the buttons were either missing or hanging from frayed threads. There was a sizable hole in the middle where

95

Duncan's fingers had ripped through the delicate silk. It was for the best. I never wanted to see it again after tonight.

"Celeste?" Vassago's voice came softly from behind me, a gentle nudge that he was there.

I turned around and handed him the garment. "Can you get rid of this for me?"

He nodded and took it between his long fingers.

"And these." I pulled off my underwear, noticing the spot of dried blood.

My bra was next. I didn't feel any less naked than I had while wearing those items of clothing. In fact, I felt more powerful standing bare in front of the man I knew would go to the ends of the Earth for me. His eyes never dipped below my face, and the welling emotions in my chest threatened to break the dam of tears.

"I'll be right on the other side of the door." He took a step back.

My arm flew out to stop him. "Leave it open."

Another cautious nod from him.

I stepped into the shower. My eyes and lips were swollen from crying, but the warm water soothed more than just my inflamed face. Duncan's stench on my skin fell to the tile and slid down the drain with the expensive unisex soap that had been sitting on the shelf.

"Do you shop for yourself?" I called out.

"No," he answered from the other room.

I wanted him closer. "What?"

"No, I don't do the shopping." His voice echoed

around me. "Is there a brand you prefer? I'll get it for you."

I peeked through the stream of suds running down my face. He was leaning against the doorjamb, his arm resting at the top of the frame. He'd taken his shirt off and put on a pair of sweatpants. My stomach fluttered.

"Who shops for you? Are there little sprites or fairies that go to the store?" I grinned and scrubbed the rest of the eucalyptus-scented shampoo out of my hair.

He smiled. "Actually, a lesser spirit in my brother's legion keeps his house in order for him. My room was primarily for guests until recently."

"Since I released you," I realized out loud.

"Since you released me." He repeated my words, but the dark sound of his voice gave them a meaning that was far different than mine.

I finished scrubbing my body then rinsed before I turned off the tap. Vassago took one large step and grabbed the towel from the counter and held it open for me. I stepped out, letting him envelop me in the plush fabric. The luxury wasn't lost on me. The whole house had more indulgence than what seemed necessary. Then again, they were princes of Hell.

"I know you have a lot of questions." He gave another intrusively knowing statement. "And I can answer them all tomorrow morning. For now, let's get you to bed."

"Where are you going to sleep?" I asked.

"I don't need to sleep."

My brows shot up to my hairline. "Ever?"

He laughed, a warm but sinister chuckle that added to his inhumanity. "I don't need to sleep tonight."

"But you do sleep, right?"

"Yes," he assured me with a dip of his chin, "but I was also slumbering in a book for a few decades, so I've been a bit restless. I'm going to read until you fall asleep."

He pointed to a large armchair that I didn't remember being there earlier, but I let that little miracle go.

"You're going to watch me sleep?"

He handed me a smaller towel for my hair then stepped back to give me space to finish drying myself off.

"No. I'm going to be reading. But if you prefer my eyes not leave you, I will oblige."

For the first time since he rescued me, his eyes trailed down my body. Most of it was covered in a white bath sheet; nonetheless, my cheeks blushed and I tightened my grip on the barrier.

"What are you reading? *Demon's Digest?*"

He snorted, and my chest swelled at the fact that I had elicited humor in a centuries-old entity.

"Actually, I'm catching up on the history of the world from my time away. Wars have come and gone. Countries formed then reformed again. I missed a lot."

Boredom, sadness, and longing mixed on his face.

I couldn't pin down why, but I wondered if he was more upset that he'd been trapped or that he'd missed the chaos.

"What year are you reading about tonight?" I stepped over to where the clothes he'd brought me sat on the counter and dropped my towel.

He opened his mouth, speechless, as I pulled a shirt over my head and down my torso. I picked up the pants and debated for a moment. It was warm on this side of the country and I was comfortable enough without them, but I'd rarely slept without pants around Duncan because he saw it as an invitation to fool around.

That made my mind up. I hugged the pants to my belly and walked toward a still-silent Vassago.

"Vass?"

The nickname snapped him out of his stupor. He moved aside but reached his hand out to my cheek.

"Vassago," he corrected. "My true name has never sounded so beautiful than when you say it."

There was a flutter of butterflies in my stomach again, but this time, it was paired with a weakness in my knees.

"Vassago?"

"Yes, my gift?"

Oh fuck. Maybe I did like his pet name for me after all. Especially when his deep, sexy voice whispered it.

"What are you going to do to Duncan after I fall asleep?"

He smiled, but his hooded eyes focused on my lips. "I've never been great with subtlety. I should have known you'd see right through me."

I shook my head. It wasn't a great leap to get to that

conclusion, but I knew I couldn't stop him from hurting or killing Duncan after what he'd done.

"It's probably better if you don't know all the gory details."

I didn't know what to say to that. A very human part of me wanted to save Duncan from the force of Hell who'd come to my aid. But a dark, primal side wanted to make him beg for death then mount his head on a pitchfork.

"I should come with you." I knew how wrong that was. I was very mortal and would be the first suspect in any sort of misfortune that befell Duncan tonight.

"You were assaulted and he left in the middle of the night. Never to be seen again after the camera outside your neighbor's door saw him walk around the corner."

As if I needed a different angle to view his proposed alibi, I tilted my head and saw his appearance quiver. It was like his whole being glitched or vibrated for the quickest moment.

I nodded, and he pressed a gentle kiss to my forehead.

CHAPTER 14
VASSAGO

The stench of my demonic form's rotting flesh filled the room when I entered it from the void. I stretched out my bony hand and pulled at the blanket on the foot of the bed. The body under it rolled and groaned with sleep.

"Celeste . . . are you there?" my victim called out.

"She is none of your concern. Rise and face punishment, putrid swine." The otherworldly voice that emitted from my skeletal mouth sent a wave of panic through the air.

"Who the fuck is there?" He scurried up to the headboard.

I salivated. It had been too long since I'd inflicted pain on one of Father's beloved humans. And longer still since I'd been the hand of retribution.

"I am your death."

I stood my ground, knowing my larger form was the wall between my prey and his only exit.

"Celeste! Oh God. Celeste, where are you?" The octave of his voice went up with every terrified word.

He bolted from the bed and dashed from one wall to another. The scent of his adrenaline and sweat seeped from his disgusting body.

I reached over to the wall next to me and turned on the light. His eyes widened in horror, and all color bleached from his face. The gruesome being standing before him was a nightmare he'd never escape.

With God-like speed, I was standing over him with my hand clamped around his neck, shutting off the scream that had been building there.

He gasped and worked his mouth like a fish on a hook.

"Neither my Father nor my gift can save you," I rasped. "Do you know what happens when you taunt the breathing embodiment of sin?"

"No. No. No." He fought against my grip, but I only tightened it until his face turned a deep shade of red.

"You become the object of my disdain. For too long, you've stood between me and my one reason for existing. Let's remedy that, shall we?"

The sounds of his struggle followed us through the void and into the wasteland where lost souls and the most depraved hellions dwelled.

Purgatory.

The pair of hellhounds at my hip gashed and snarled, the thick chains around their necks strung tight in my grasp. I'd borrowed them from a duke who said they were thirsty for blood. They'd been caged, watching as I tortured Duncan when we'd first arrived. A motley of pained wails and snuffs of impatient growling had set the tone perfectly, but now it was the beasts' turn and they were ravenous.

There would be nothing left of him.

Duncan's blood trailed from the post he'd been bound to. To give my accomplices an unfair advantage, I'd fileted the skin from his chest and shoulder with a dull blade. I'd let him run for an hour before getting the pooches ready for their hunt.

The hellhound on my left sniffed the air and snapped its jaw.

"Ready or not . . ." I let go of both chains.

The hellhounds ran toward a line of trees on the edge of a swamp. The misty terrain didn't slow them down, but I had to rely on the sounds of screaming to know whether they'd caught up to Duncan.

When I reached the scene, the hounds had descended on Duncan's legs. The flesh had been torn away, revealing bare bones and snapped tendons.

I held up my hand and the carnage stopped. Both mutts growled, the muscles in their shoulders tense, ready to finish their feast.

Duncan was shaking. He was close to going into shock and was losing all of his remaining blood as his heart betrayed him by pumping as hard as it could. His gaze panned unsteadily up at me.

"Why are you doing this? Please don't kill me. Please!" he screamed through the pain. "Who are you?"

I took hold of his sweat- and blood-soaked hair. His sobbing wails turned to understanding when my face changed to resemble one he was more familiar with. He shook his head in disbelief.

"I am a worse threat than you'd imagined. This is your just reward for the unspeakable crimes you've committed." I lifted his head and forced his eyes on the obedient hounds waiting for my signal. "And they are hungry." His whole body quaked, but I held firm. "You forced your filth on my gift. I will baptize her in your blood as she comes on my tongue."

I took the blade from my pocket and plunged it into his carotid artery. I pulled it out quickly then filled a small jar with the crimson liquid that pumped from his body until it slowed. His eyes rolled back. He was slipping away from consciousness.

With that, I let him fall to the ground, snapped my fingers, and watched as the beasts tore into his belly as he screamed the bloody murder he was being subjected to. His entrails covered the ground and soon, the last of his strained voice faded away to the grunts and crunch of razor-sharp teeth on wet bone.

I debated cleaning myself before stepping back into the house in Malibu, but something in me needed to show Celeste that the deed was done. Her monster had been slain, and I bore the proof on my hands, bare chest, and face.

My bed was empty when I stepped through the void, but she hadn't gone far.

She sat with her knees to her chest in the armchair, wrapped in the comforter. "You're back?"

Her wide eyes took me in, but her face remained stony. It was one thing for humans to wish death on one another, but it was more sobering to see the remnants of it on my skin.

"I'm sorry I was gone when you woke. I intended to be back sooner."

"Is he . . . ?"

"He will never be able to hurt anyone else ever again."

The tension in her shoulders loosened slightly. Killing Duncan wouldn't take away the pain he'd inflicted on her for far too long, but she was the shining knight who slayed the dragon. I was merely her sword.

She got to her feet and took a step closer to me, then two more until she was only inches away. My hands twitched around the jar I'd brought with me. I wanted to run my blood-stained thumb over her lips. The thin material of my T-shirt covering her body did nothing to hide her taut nipples.

"Thank you." She didn't shy away, and there was an edge of power in her tone.

"I would do anything for you, my gift."

The blood on my body became her focus. The dark, rusty color of it made my skin ruddy and dry, but the tacky liquid trapped in my fists was still fresh. I hadn't lied to Duncan when I said I wanted to wash his sins from Celeste's soul with his blood.

Her eyes rolled up to mine. "What is that?"

I brought the vessel up. "Do you trust me?"

CHAPTER 15
CELESTE

Did I trust him?

He was joking, wasn't he?

The question burned between us.

I should be scared staring into the eyes of Duncan's killer, but the blood splattered on his sharp cheekbones only made him look more dangerously beautiful. The dark stains across his chest and the distinct marks that looked like Duncan had put up a fight and lost made my blood warm.

Maybe I was more ruthless than I'd ever thought. I needed to be competitive in my male-dominated field of study. If a colleague asked for help, I would point them in the right direction but would never get involved personally unless I was paired with them. Liam was my research partner, but when it came time for the fellowship to be announced, I would not clap and say that he deserved it more than I did.

But would I kill for the spot?

That was a question I should have asked myself when I wished for the fellowship in that basement.

Being the reason for Duncan's death had nothing to do with school or our careers.

He raped me.

He took a part of me that I could never get back.

Even though I knew Vassago had finished the job, I would look for Duncan in the dark for years to come. That realization made me want to wrap the demon around me and carry him everywhere I went.

That was what Vassago had been offering me, though, wasn't it?

"My gift?" His wary tone took me out of my busy brain.

"Yes. I trust you." My voice sounded weak, but I couldn't remember the last time I'd been more grateful or trusted someone more.

He opened the jar of blood—it was definitely blood by the metallic smell—and dipped his middle finger into the inky fluid. "Pull your shirt down."

His eyes didn't leave mine as I curled my fingers around the neckline and didn't stop until the swells of my breasts were exposed.

His lips parted and his gaze dropped to his canvas. Something squirmed in my belly at the determined look he held with every swipe of his fingers over my bare skin.

Slowly, he painted the first long line down the center of my chest. The next line started at one breast and crossed to the other. He refreshed his morbid paint and drew the boxy beetle I'd seen time and time again. When he finished, he took one step back to survey his work.

"What does it mean?" I asked.

"That you're mine."

My mouth snapped shut.

"This symbol is my true name. My sigil on the skin of my most beloved and cherished gift."

I blushed, but his only reaction came from the way his eyelids lowered and he wet his lips. He looked like the quintessential bad boy in every classic film.

"It's only fair that I mark you as mine. Don't you think?"

Before he could answer, I plunged two fingers into the jar of Duncan's blood. Vassago stood as still as a statue while I scrawled my name across his muscular chest. Holding the neck of my shirt firm so his masterpiece was still on full display, I wet my fingers every other letter. The trail of blood dripped down to my elbow and stained the oversized sleeve. By the time I got to the last *e* in my name, my hand and wrist were slick and sticky.

I rested my hand on his stomach while I waited for his reaction. He looked down at my markings, then at my fingers.

"Thank you." He sounded more than grateful. He sounded whole.

I cupped his cheek with my clean hand. His eyes met mine, and an inferno ignited in my core. I had already pushed the boundaries of what I was capable of tonight, but I pulled his mouth to mine.

Sparks.

Butterflies.

A thousand yellow daisies exploded inside of me.

His soft lips moved over mine, then his tongue teased at the seam. When I opened for him, he didn't just deepen our kiss. It was as if my soul were exploring a home it had been missing. The sweet taste of him fueled the fire already burning inside of me.

I was still sore from Duncan's attack. The bruises on my wrists were only hours old. But if I didn't get closer to Vassago, I might die from overheating.

My slippery fingers fumbled at the button of his jeans.

"You need time," he said with a hand on top of mine as I got them loose. He pulled away and gently gripped my chin. "It's too soon after—"

"You said you would give me anything I wanted." I fixed him with a determined gaze and pulled at the waistband of his boxers.

I needed to extend the feeling of control that was pushing me through the pain and devastation, which would surely return in the morning.

In that moment, I needed to have a say about who was inside of me.

He kicked his head back with a frustrated rumble in his chest. "Celeste, I am not going to be able to restrain myself if you say things like that. I'm trying to be what you deserve."

But my thumbs were already pushing his pants past the notches of his hips and letting them fall to his feet. His cock was hard and at attention, much like every other part of him.

I pulled my T-shirt over my head and added it to the pool of clothing around us.

He sucked in a breath as my hand wrapped around his silky shaft. "Fuck," he breathed.

"I am not broken, Vassago."

I pumped him once, and his head snapped down to watch. Another slow stroke brought a bead of arousal to his tip, and I swiped my thumb over it. His fluid mixed with the blood still coating my hand.

"There is nothing wrong with taking things slow after you experienced what you did." He was trying to reason with me, but I refused all reason.

"You're a little bit past being morally right, don't you think?" I squeezed the head of his cock again, but he put his hand over mine, stopping me midstroke.

"I would live in madness if it meant being at your side."

"Then let me be the one to decide what's too much for me. Give into my madness for the night. Please."

He leaned down to kiss me but didn't remove his hand until I'd removed mine. His arm wrapped around my back to pull me against him. The marks on our bare chests smudged together as I stood on the tips of my toes to get as close to him as I could.

"Vassago," I begged, the aching between my legs turning from need to pain.

He finally groaned in defeat and hauled me into him. My legs wrapped around his hips while he turned us toward his bed. My fingers weaved through his hair. I wanted to memorize the feel of him with every sensory organ I had. I traced his lips with my tongue.

"If you want power, there is no better place for it than on top of me."

I giggled over his mouth as he sat down on the edge of the bed. His cock pressed to my belly, and I wanted nothing more than to feel him inside of me. When I pulled away from him, my arm knocked the forgotten blood out of his hand, spilling it between us.

He didn't miss a beat. He tossed the jar aside and pulled me deeper into his lap to kiss me—hard. The desperation mounted and he lifted me just enough for the head of his cock to nudge at the entrance of my pussy. The viscous liquid squelched between our bodies as I eased down his shaft and then back up again, taking all of him inside of me.

My breath hitched. The deep angle hit all the right spots at once.

I felt an orgasm building in my belly, but his arms around my waist tightened, slowing my pace.

"Oh, please," I breathed through another bounce of my body on his. "I'm so close."

He pulled us farther up the bed until his head rested against the wooden slats of the headboard. In this new position, I could see the way his eyes sparkled as he watched me ride him. His hands roamed my body until he cupped my breasts, his fingers pinching my hard nipples.

I clung to the top of the headboard as his thrusts met my hips' cadence. His fingers twisted, and the sharp pain sent a burst of pleasure from my core to my fingers and toes. My moans filled the room, accompanied by the slapping of his slick thighs against my ass while he held my hips tight in place, rutting into me from below.

A new orgasm was already starting to take hold in my core when he said, "Look at me."

I did as he demanded, though I could hardly focus.

"Tell me that you're mine."

"I'm yours," I whined as he dragged out of me to his tip then rammed back inside to the hilt.

"Again," he demanded with his words and cock.

"I'm yours."

Another blow of his hips. "Again," he ground out through his teeth.

"I'm yours!"

"That's right." He pulled me down and rolled my hips over his. "And whose cock is this?"

"Mine?" I followed the pressure of his hands on my waist.

"You command me, gift. Say it louder." He increased the speed, and my body reacted. "Whose cock is this?"

"Mine." *Oh fuck.*

"Fuck yes, it is."

He let out a thick groan and worked my hips harder,

sending me so far into ecstasy that I wasn't sure I was going to come down. Every nerve in my body buzzed with my final orgasm.

I collapsed on his chest.

We stayed there a moment, his fingers tracing a light path up and down my spine until the aftershocks stopped firing through my limbs. Later, when we showered the blood and other fluids from our skin, he scrubbed me off with tender hands. His touch was addictive.

We tucked ourselves into fresh blankets that appeared like magic. Vassago pulled me onto his bare chest and refused to let go. It was the most restful sleep I could remember.

CHAPTER 16
VASSAGO

Reluctantly, I took Celeste back to her townhouse the next morning. We packed and moved her belongings into an apartment I decided to rent that was closer to her school. Duncan had demanded that the lease on the townhouse be solely in his name. Another aspect of constant control.

The demon who owned the apartment building refused to take my money, but we needed forged proof that Celeste had been planning to leave Duncan before he'd gone missing. And he was now considered as much. No one had seen hide or hair of him in over forty-eight hours.

The plan was to make it look like he'd gone missing between the townhouse and the train station. His things were already in the beginning stages of packing for his impending move to Boston, and it wasn't difficult to manipulate the footage taken by the neighbor's door camera. From their vantage point, a figure that was

Duncan's height and build was seen leaving in the middle of the night with one piece of luggage trailing behind him.

Celeste told the police that they'd had a fight and that he'd refused to stay one more minute in their condo. The upstairs neighbor confirmed that there were several arguments downstairs that night. What the woman didn't know was that the first was Duncan assaulting my precious Celeste and the following was me exacting revenge.

Duncan's suitcase was found on the side of the road a few miles away from the train depot. I'd left the zipper undone for a more dramatic effect. His clothing had been strewn about, but his wallet and passport were amongst his belongings.

No trace of him would be found, but when others were questioned about him, it came out that he had raped all three of his last girlfriends before storming off and blaming them for his indiscretions.

A pattern that I felt had a just ending.

Celeste didn't confess to the assault when asked. She wasn't ready to admit or relive it. I didn't push her. She still felt guilty for not coming forward to add to the charges he would never face, but Duncan being classified as a missing suspect in three sexual assaults was reason enough for his disappearance. The nightmares of him on top of her plagued her enough. I almost wished I hadn't killed him so quickly. When my gift woke up frightened, I wanted nothing more than to strangle the life out of him again.

Seere and Gaap had kept their end of our bargain already. One of Celeste's cohort members had been arrested for starting a bar brawl that put two people in the hospital. He was suspended from academics until the legal matters were settled. If he was permitted to return, it would be long after the fellowship started.

Shortly after that change was announced, Gaap struck. The student he targeted was inspired to quit school entirely to pursue a life of pleasure. With his trust fund, he skipped off to a small island in the South Pacific.

I had the gratification of taking down James Hannigan. It was hard to do. He did nothing but study and attend classes. But with a flush of envy, he went into a jealous rage about anyone being considered his equal. He threw a tantrum during his last presentation, which resulted in his rejection from the fellowship and chronic embarrassment that would follow him for the rest of his life.

Now, Celeste was pacing the floor of our living room as I battled the new bookcase I was tasked with installing. I'd promised this woman a home library in the spare bedroom, and it was only missing a few more shelves.

"They'll call," I assured her.

"But they should have called an hour ago. Maybe they found out that I—"

"Made a deal with a demon who worships the ground you walk on for a position in the fellowship? I highly doubt it." I peeked around the manufactured wood panels to see her scrunching her nose at me.

"I deserve to be accepted," she said more to herself.

I screwed in the stabilizer and walked back to the living room, where she was staring down at her blank phone screen.

"Yes. You do." I pushed her device aside and bent down to hook my arms under her legs. Celeste squealed as I hauled her up to wrap her thighs around me. "They are just letting everyone else down easy. Now, where is that heinously tiny L-thing."

The Swedish company swore anyone could put their furniture together within twenty minutes. And they said Lucifer was the master of mistruths.

"It's an Allen wrench. Silly Hell-dweller."

"Sass me again and I'll dwell between your legs for the rest of the day with no mercy." Her cheeks flushed, but she pulled the ridiculous tool from her pocket. "Always holding on to everything I need." I nuzzled her neck and took a deep lungful of the perfume on her heated skin. My cock hardened against her center, and her hips rolled.

"You're trying to distract me."

I met her hooded gaze. "Do you want me to? Because I'm starved for a taste."

She shivered. I pulled at the top of her sundress and licked up her collarbone to the succulent flesh at the crook of her neck.

Her phone rang, and she held it up to her ear with wide eyes. "Hello?" she answered. "Yes."

I watched her facial expressions carefully. Her brows furrowed and her lips pursed as the person on the other line spoke. My grip on her tightened, but she was as still as death, hanging on every word.

Finally, her face lit up. "I accept. Yes. I will see you at orientation. Thank you." She tapped the screen and threw her hands up in the air. "I GOT IT!"

Pure pride filled my whole body. "You got it!"

She cupped my face for a long, deep kiss. I took a step into our bedroom, avoiding the small tower of boxes by the door.

Unpacking and building bookshelves would have to wait.

Her hands pulled at my shirt but moved to the buttons on my jeans when I dropped her on the undone bed. I had her this morning, but it was never enough.

I pulled my shirt over my head, and her eyes met mine as she pushed my pants and boxers to the ground. Her hand wrapped around my cock, and she flicked her tongue over the tip.

I groaned for more.

She pumped me agonizingly slowly as her lips puckered over my tip while she sucked. "Why are you torturing me? Let me celebrate you."

Her cheeks hollowed and then her lips gave a loud pop when she released me. "This isn't torture." She smiled wickedly. "I know exactly how to do that."

"Any moment I'm forced to not be buried inside of you is torture," I retorted.

She lay back on the bed and pulled the hem of her

dress up to her bare pussy. My mouth watered as I dropped to my knees. She rested her foot on my shoulder, stopping me from coming any closer as her finger worked her clit for me to watch.

Her pleasure belonged to me. A wave of lust and jealousy washed over me while two of her fingers dipped between her glistening lips. That sweet arousal should only cover my tongue.

"Mmm," she moaned, the pads of her fingers circling what was mine. "Feels so good."

Her back arched and her other hand came down with a small vibrating toy we'd used this morning. The low buzz quickened her breath as she massaged it over her clit.

"Oh fuck yes," she breathed.

I groaned and fisted my cock.

"I'm going to come." Her body tensed which broke the tether of my restraint.

My hands gripped her thighs, pulling her down to my mouth in one quick motion.

"The fuck you are." My gruff voice was muffled by her wet pussy. "Not unless I'm the one to savor it."

Pushing her hands away, I domed my mouth over her clit, plunging two fingers into her. Her walls pulsed around me as I sucked, licked, and devoured her. She screamed my name as the orgasm overtook her.

I crawled up between her legs, taking in the look on her face when I eased the tip of my cock inside. Her body was still coming down from the high. Her euphoria and the power she knew she held over me gave her an irresistible glow.

My cock slammed into her wet heat, and I took her mouth with mine, letting her taste herself on my lips. With another hard thrust, she wrapped her arms around my neck to keep me close.

"Harder," she demanded.

I did. Her hips circled, searching for the friction she needed to come again.

"Vass," she whined.

"Vassago." I pulled out to the tip then dove deep again.

"Vassago!"

"Whose pussy is this?" I grunted, rutting into her.

"Only yours." Her low, needy voice in my ear was too much. "I'm yours."

"Mine."

I lost myself in her. The sounds of our pleasure filled the room until we were both spent and left panting, wrapped in the sweat-damp sheets.

Nothing would ever be more perfect in any life I would ever live.

Her fingers made small circles on my chest, and her brown eyes stared into mine. I could spend hours memorizing each striation of her irises. The way the light hit them to reveal their rich earth tones.

"I love you." She said it softly, almost hesitantly, as if I wouldn't move Heaven and Hell for her.

I rolled to my side and pulled her in tight. Words could not convey or contain the love I had for this woman. Every speck of my being and hers had been made to fit together on this plane, at this very moment, in a vast eternity. Every sun in every galaxy only burned to bring us together.

Nothing felt big or small enough.

So instead, I pressed my lips to her and said, "I love you, my Celeste."

My gift.

CHAPTER 17

CELESTE

Who would have known that stealing a book from the library would change my entire world so wholly?

Every piece of the puzzle had fallen into place, and I was happier than I ever knew possible. I was also exhausted. Something about Vassago awoke a sexual appetite in me that was insatiable. Between hours of studying, I was on my knees or bent over a chair in the library. At night, I lost sleep just to be worshiped for hours. He touched me in places I never knew would arouse me and taught me things about my sensuality that no other lover had.

Vassago had granted me more than my academic goals. He was a walking wealth of knowledge and had lived through events that most historians would only be able to speculate on. Secrets that had been lost to time were easily dug up in his memory. He was a walking wealth of knowledge.

Vassago was still territorial and showed his true nature at times. The motorcycle he'd evidently stolen was only the start of how thirsty he was for the fine things others possessed. But keeping his focus was as easy as snapping my fingers and lifting my top. He rarely threatened to kill anyone, but he quickly showed people—Liam specifically—who owned my heart, body, and soul.

Only because I allowed it.

I loved that man.

That demon.

He spoke of our love like it was his greatest longing. The years trapped in the book had been worth his solitude because I was the first thing he saw when released. And in a way, I had also been trapped in a life I'd made.

We'd both been freed, and there was nothing in this world or any other that could come between us. He would never let it.

My protector and champion.

My Vassago.

CHAPTER 18
VASSAGO

Living with Celeste was the peak of domesticity. She spent her days in class and at the library, and when her day was done—and my watch was over—I cooked us dinner. Never mind that I had been dodging Seere's and Gaap's calls since the night Celeste had summoned me to her rescue. But I was out of excuses when there was a knock on the door after I'd put Celeste to bed with a book and hot tea.

"Did you invite someone over?" She came out into the hall and stared at the source of the intrusion.

I rubbed the back of my neck. "I believe it's time that I introduce you to my brothers." I pulled the door open and, to no surprise, standing in the hallway were Gaap and Seere.

"Sorry to have missed the housewarming party," Seere snarked. "Our invite must have gotten lost."

I furrowed my brow in mocking disdain then pulled him in for a hug. "You better have brought a present."

"Good to see you, too, brother." Seere stepped into the kitchen and made room for Gaap to come in behind him.

Gaap was not alone. His human companion clung to his side as he nodded to me in greeting. "This is my wife, Pru," he announced. "Pru, this is the Prince of Envy."

I stole a look behind me at Celeste, who seemed more surprised about my title than the two demons on her doorstep.

Pru rolled her eyes, obviously exhausted by being dragged to middle-of-the-night family meetings. "How many brothers do you have?"

"Six." Gaap beamed at me.

"I promise Vassago isn't as bad as Oro," Seere interjected.

Pru laughed and snapped her wit back at him "Is he as bad as you? Oro is a puppy compared to the prissy Prince of Wrath."

"Vass is his own brand of ruthless." Seere grinned darkly, and I heard a squeak from my Celeste.

"Hmm." Pru surveyed me once more. "From what I can see, as long as he has this babe behind him, he's just as whipped as Oro."

They all shared a chuckle, and I shut the door behind them then ushered everyone into the living room.

I pulled Celeste under my arm, and she looked up at me. Thousands of questions swirled in her eyes, but there would be time for that later.

Pru bounded forward and extended her hand to Celeste. With the most charming smile, she said, "I'm really glad to meet you, Celeste. Do you mind if I grab a glass of water? The void is dry and always leaves me parched."

Celeste gave her a small, grateful smile and took her hand. "Nice to meet you too. I think I need something stronger than water for this. Wine?"

"I actually don't drink, but I know these guys won't turn you down. Do you have whiskey?"

"God, yes."

Together, they turned into the kitchen with Gaap calling behind them, "Don't bring Father into this, beautiful."

Pru stuck her tongue out over her shoulder at him.

I leaned against the wall, my arms crossed and waiting for the scolding I was sure they were here to deliver.

Pru and Celeste came back with several glasses, a bottle of bourbon that Seere had sent me, and two soft drinks. Celeste set everything on the coffee table then started pouring everyone a drink. She brought one to me and took one for herself before allowing me to drape an arm around her.

"*Skål.*" Seere raised his glass then downed half in one gulp.

Everyone followed.

"Right. Now down to business." Seere set his glass down with a loud clink then clapped his hands together.

I narrowed my eyes at him.

"What business?" Celeste looked up at me for the answer.

I took a deep breath, trying to calm my aggravation.

"We need your book, hun," Pru said. She was perched on Gaap's lap as his hand smoothed up and down her thigh.

"My book?" Celeste looked between my brothers and Pru. "The one I found Vassago in? Why do you need that?"

Seere answered, "That book you released my brother from is part of a set. The owners of the others have a little vendetta against the forces of Hell, and we would like to level the playing field a bit."

Celeste's brow furrowed. "What does that mean?"

"Those diaries contain spells, charms, and other magical objects that have been passed down from generation to generation within the Order of Exorcists," Gaap explained carefully. "The Order used the diaries through the centuries to hunt witches, demons, and other creatures of the dark. But now, their main focus is on us. The princes of Hell."

Celeste was quiet a moment. I knew her heart longed to dissect the text and keep the rare find for further study. It was priceless and full of history that humans rarely got a peek at, but she'd also found me in its pages. What else would she discover in the weathered parchments?

"You just want the book?" she asked.

"And perhaps some help translating if things get dicey later," Seere added.

"Are you going to hurt them?" Celeste retreated farther into my side, a silent bid for a way out of the implication.

I pulled her chin up to face me. "No more than they've hurt us."

Realization dawned in her eyes. It would be retaliation for my fifty-year isolation.

"These priests have no mercy. They're fighting a war that no one on either side called for in the name of a Father who has condemned them." Gaap's voice pulled Celeste's attention from me. "I would not be here today if it weren't for Pru. So, yes. To keep Vassago safe, we will need that book."

He pulled Pru off his lap and plopped her on the seat next to Seere. Celeste tensed next to me but showed no fear when he came to stand in front of her.

"As the princes of Hell, we shouldn't have to ask this of you. It isn't part of the mortal design to interfere with our existence on this plane. But if you'd like to keep the man who has won your heart, then this is the way to do so. Because they're coming. For all of us. And they will kill whoever is by our side."

He looked back at Pru, who was absently rubbing her wrist. "I've promised to spend every moment of my existence loving and taking care of Pru, just as Vassago has to you," he continued. "I need this favor from you to keep my word."

I knew he'd said exactly what Celeste needed to hear. She nodded then walked to our bedroom. A moment later, she came out clutching the book to her chest.

"You're going to use it to survive? Not hurt innocents?" She needed the lines in the sand drawn.

"No one is innocent, darling." Seere made a show of dragging his eyes over her body.

She was wearing a silk pajama set. The shorts were short, but not as risqué as his insinuation was.

"Seere," I said in warning. The only one he would get.

His rakish smile did little to convince me that he was done goading me or Celeste.

"I love it when you get angry, Vass." Seere rolled his head on the couch cushion then looked at me again. "Reminds me of the good ol' days. Remember that plague we started a few centuries back? You were rapacious. Your hair was also much longer."

"How is that helping assure her that the Order of Exorcists is the enemy?" Gaap scolded our brother.

"Hey, no one forced them to drink the holy Flavor-Aid," Seere said. "But she should know who she's getting in bed with."

Celeste squared her shoulders. "I know who you are. I'm not blind to Vassago's power."

Seere's eyes met mine, and a knowing smile spread across his face. "I bet you do."

"Fine." Celeste shoved the book in Seere's hands, clearly as annoyed with him as I was.

Seere yelped in pain and jumped up from the

couch. The book dropped to the floor. "What the fuck was that?"

Celeste swooped it up again, tucking it close to her body.

Gaap laughed. "Oh right. Forgot to warn you about that. Those have a bit of a bite to them."

"You asshole," Seere said into his hands, which were bubbling with blisters.

"I'll handle that, hun," Pru offered.

Celeste looked between Gaap, Seere, and me. "I want it back. In one piece."

Gaap nodded and stepped back to give the book a wide berth. "We will do our best to document each page as we go. Just in case something does happen, we'll have some sort of copy. As long as the thing doesn't burst into flame on its own, it will be returned to you."

"And everything inside?" Celeste quickly added her caveat.

"I can't promise that. Some things aren't meant to be accessible to mortals or exist on this plane."

Celeste's eyes fell to the top of the book. The lumpy thing was full of trinkets that would have given many people nightmares, but to Celeste, they were artifacts. The tome was a window into a whole world she didn't know existed until now.

"My gift?" I came to her side and rested a hand on her lower back. "Please."

She nodded, gave its cover one last caress, and handed it over to Pru, who promptly hugged it to her as a promise to keep it safe.

"Thanks," Pru said. "I think you and I will be great friends. I'll give you my number before we go, okay?" Pru's gentle nature eased my Celeste's shoulders, and I was more than grateful for that.

"All right. One more drink, then it's time for us to head back to our own coast," Gaap announced, swiping the bottle of whiskey by the neck and filling three of the glasses once more.

After one drink turned into four, I watched Celeste laugh and listen carefully to the stories that Gaap and Seere told. My gift was welcomed by the family that had never given up on me. What was likely a small gesture to them was more than I could have asked for.

Celeste silently checked in when my brothers started to get carried away with their tales of grandeur. Pru piped in as quick as a whip to put Gaap in his place when he boasted about the women he'd famously seduced throughout the centuries. Seere hooted with laughter at how trained he thought Gaap and I were, but neither of us was bothered. Gaap may have not known how deflecting those comments were since Seere was as tame as a kitten for a human who he'd been chasing for years.

That wasn't my story to tell, but as I lounged back with Celeste tucked into my side on the couch, I knew I'd found happiness. Delirious joy. Ravenous love. And most of all, peace.

What could be more satisfying on this plane than finding the person who not only made you whole, but made you happy to be alive?

. . .

THE END

Wicked

Ab-session

1 oz Gin

1 oz Grapefruit Juice

1 oz Grand Marnier

1 oz Dry Vermouth

1/2-3/4 tsp Absinthe (full

tsp if your extra spicy)

Candied orange peel and

orange wedge for garnish

Acknowledgments

The list of people who helped ease me into my darker side is a mile long. But a special thanks has to go to Allie Stern and Ayden Perry for not only being my late night writing friends but giving me their insight on the darker elements.

Thank you to my editor, Caroline. I will never be able to thank you enough for being in my head the way you have always been.

Speaking of knowing my brain all too well, thank you Norma Gambini for not only proofreading every one of these books but for just "getting it".

As always, to my wifey. A. K. Mulford, you are my rock. I can't imagine this life without you.

Thank you to my PA, Leah, for just being my second brain. I don't think I could have made it through this year without you.

I'm so lucky to have so many fantastic people in my life!

Made in the USA
Columbia, SC
26 September 2024

43060054R00095